S

P9-CPW-537

Praise for Anna Schmidt

"Schmidt pens a wonderful love story."
—*RT Book Reviews* on *A Convenient Wife*

"Schmidt's characters are witty, charming, mysterious and worth getting to know."
—*RT Book Reviews* on *An Unexpected Suitor*

"Schmidt knows what readers expect in a love story and delivers on all levels. It's refreshing to see characters with their flaws showing, which makes them appear very real."
—*RT Book Reviews* on *Gift from the Sea*

"Reminiscent of a fairy tale. It's a charming, sweet story with a beautiful ending."
—*RT Book Reviews* on *Seaside Cinderella*

Praise for Linda Ford

"A tender, sweet love story with characters who only want the best for others and themselves."
—*RT Book Reviews* on *Dakota Cowboy*

"Ford's sweet, charming love story has well-written characters that demonstrate strong faith, even though they stumble along the way."
—*RT Book Reviews* on *The Cowboy's Baby*

"*The Journey Home* is a splendid tale of love, hope and faith, not only with ourselves but also with God."
—*RT Book Reviews*

ANNA SCHMIDT

is an award-winning author of more than twenty-five works of historical and contemporary fiction. She is a two-time finalist for a coveted RITA® Award from Romance Writers of America, as well as four times a finalist for an *RT Book Reviews* Reviewers' Choice Award. Her most recent *RT Book Reviews* Reviewers' Choice nomination was for her 2008 Love Inspired Historical novel *Seaside Cinderella*, which is the first of a series of four historical novels set on the romantic island of Nantucket. Critics have called Anna "a natural writer, spinning tales reminiscent of old favorites like *Miracle on 34th Street*." Her characters have been called "realistic" and "endearing" and one reviewer raved, "I love Anna Schmidt's style of writing!"

LINDA FORD

shares her life with her rancher husband, a grown son, a live-in client she provides care for, and a yappy parrot. She and her husband raised a family of fourteen children, ten adopted, providing her with plenty of opportunity to experience God's love and faithfulness. They had their share of adventures, as well. Taking twelve kids in a motor home on a three-thousand-mile road trip would be high on the list. They live in Alberta, Canada, close enough to the Rockies to admire them every day. She enjoys writing stories that reveal God's wondrous love through the lives of her characters.

Linda enjoys hearing from readers. Contact her at linda@lindaford.org or check out her website at www.lindaford.org, where you can also catch her blog, which often carries glimpses of both her writing activities and family life.

ANNA SCHMIDT
LINDA FORD

Christmas Under Western Skies

Steeple
Hill®

Published by Steeple Hill Books™

If you purchased this book without a cover you should be aware that this book is stolen property. It was reported as "unsold and destroyed" to the publisher, and neither the author nor the publisher has received any payment for this "stripped book."

STEEPLE HILL BOOKS

Steeple
Hill®

Recycling programs
for this product may
not exist in your area.

ISBN-13: 978-0-373-82850-0

CHRISTMAS UNDER WESTERN SKIES

Copyright © 2010 by Harlequin Books S.A.

The publisher acknowledges the copyright holders of the individual works as follows:

A PRAIRIE FAMILY CHRISTMAS
Copyright © 2010 by Jo Horne Schmidt

A COWBOY'S CHRISTMAS
Copyright © 2010 by Linda Ford

All rights reserved. Except for use in any review, the reproduction or utilization of this work in whole or in part in any form by any electronic, mechanical or other means, now known or hereafter invented, including xerography, photocopying and recording, or in any information storage or retrieval system, is forbidden without the written permission of the editorial office, Steeple Hill Books, 233 Broadway, New York, NY 10279 U.S.A.

This is a work of fiction. Names, characters, places and incidents are either the product of the author's imagination or are used fictitiously, and any resemblance to actual persons, living or dead, business establishments, events or locales is entirely coincidental.

This edition published by arrangement with Steeple Hill Books.

® and TM are trademarks of Steeple Hill Books, used under license. Trademarks indicated with ® are registered in the United States Patent and Trademark Office, the Canadian Trade Marks Office and in other countries.

www.SteepleHill.com

Printed in U.S.A.

CONTENTS

A PRAIRIE FAMILY CHRISTMAS
Anna Schmidt

To dear friends who have known the loss of a first love and made the journey from grief to acceptance with grace and great dignity.

Only take heed to thyself and keep thy soul diligently, lest thou forget the things which thine eyes have seen, and lest they depart from thy heart all the days of thy life.

—*Deuteronomy* 4:9

Chapter One

❧

Homestead, Dakota Territories
Late October, 1865

Julianne Cooper coaxed her ox, Dusty, over the rutted and snow-covered path that connected her farm to that of Glory and Sam Foster. The Fosters were freed slaves who had—like Julianne and her late husband, Luke—taken advantage of the Homestead Act of 1862 and headed west to claim their one hundred and sixty acres. The dozen families that had settled in the area had already established a thriving community that they had named "Homestead."

"You should head back, Sam," Julianne called to her friend walking alongside the wagon. "It'll be dark soon and Glory will worry."

Her son, Luke, Jr., had run ahead searching for dried, frozen buffalo chips to stoke the fire when they got home. His twin, Laura, sat huddled under a buffalo robe next to Julianne.

"Mama!"

Luke's cry of alarm had Sam running as Julianne halted the wagon and slid from the seat, sinking in slush that covered her shoes when she landed. "Stay here," she ordered her daughter. "Luke! Are you hurt?"

The boy did not reply, just pointed.

Near the grove of bur oak trees that her late husband had designated as the perfect setting for their house stood a riderless horse, saddled and loaded with gear.

"Can we keep him?" Luke asked.

"Go back to the wagon and stay with your sister," Julianne ordered.

Her mind raced with possibilities—none of them good. Over time, most of the Indians in the area had been moved to reservations by the government. The few who remained had come to accept the reality of settlers from the east; but still, every now and again there were stories of renegades. Or it could be a trap. Some poacher come to claim her land for himself. Or…

"Over here," Sam called and knelt next to a lifeless form half covered over with drifted snow.

Julianne stumbled through patches of frozen high grass stalks. "Is he…"

"Not yet," Sam replied as he hoisted the man over one shoulder as if he were no more than a sack of flour. "But we'd best get him inside and warmed up or he surely will be."

Julianne considered their choices. They could turn

the wagon and head back to the Fosters. But Glory was sick in bed. And Julianne's place was closer. Sam eased the man into the back of the wagon and then went back for the horse.

"I'll go with you," he said, mounting the horse.

Julianne nodded and climbed back onto the wagon, her skirt wet and heavy now.

"Is that man dead?" Luke asked, squirming around to study the form in the back.

"Not yet," Julianne replied through gritted teeth.

Captain Nathan Cook faded in and out of consciousness. One minute he was aware of sliding to the frozen ground from Salt's back, and the next he felt the bone-jarring motion of a wagon making its way slowly over uneven ground. One minute he opened his eyes to see an elderly black man riding Salt, and the next he was sure he heard a woman quietly giving orders as he was moved from the wagon and into a dark, close room that smelled of smoke and damp earth. One minute he was so cold that he was beyond shivering, to stir the embers of inner warmth his body might still provide, and the next he was buried under a soft pelt of dank fur. One minute he was tempted to give himself over to the blessedness of everlasting sleep, and the next he was following orders barked at him like his command officer once had, only these came with a feminine drawl.

"Mister? Open your eyes. Mister? Look at me. Who are you? Where were you heading?"

There was no tolerance for disobedience in that

command, no matter how sweet the voice, so Nathan did as she ordered and forced his eyes open. He found himself staring straight into the eyes of what was surely one of God's most beautiful angels.

"California," he murmured, choosing to answer the question that was simplest. Then he closed his eyes again and gave himself over to his fate.

For two days the man lay close to death. But in spite of Sam's thinly veiled hints that Julianne should think about where and how they might bury him and get word back to his people of his passing, Julianne refused to even consider the idea that this man would die in her house.

It never occurred to her that what she was really fighting were the memories of her husband's death, and yet the similarities were astounding. Like this man, Luke had gone out in a storm. Like this man, he had become disoriented. Like this man, by the time they found him he was wracked with fever and at the same time half-frozen.

"This isn't Big Luke," Glory warned her the next day, when she arrived with the ingredients to mix up a generous helping of her special plaster for drawing out fever.

"I know that," Julianne whispered, mindful of her children not ten feet away. Hopefully, Sam had distracted them enough with his game of shadow figures that they had momentarily forgotten about the man lying where they had last seen their father. Even at noon, the house was dark enough for the game.

"It's not the same at all, but for them..." She jerked her head in the direction of the children as she helped Glory lift the man's upper body so they could wrap the strips of torn cotton around the plaster Glory had spread over his bare chest.

He was muscular but too thin, as if it had been some time since he'd had a decent meal. Glory helped her ease the man back onto the cornhusk mattress, then stood with hands on hips and glanced toward the wooden table that dominated the center of the small room. "You make anything of those papers he was carrying?"

"His name is Nathan Cook. He was a captain in the Confederate Army. There's a letter of honorable discharge from General Lee and a paper that shows ownership of his horse. There's a picture of him in uniform and another of a young woman—perhaps it's his wife or sister."

Glory frowned. "A southern boy? Way out here?" Glory's expression shifted from concern to wariness. "That can't be good." She stared at the items Julianne had spread out over the table to dry and fingered a small leather-covered Bible. "This was part of his belongings?"

Julianne nodded. "And that journal as well."

Glory picked up the second volume and studied it. "Did you read it?"

"No."

"Read it," Glory instructed. "Folks will lie to your face, but when they write down their thinking, that's something you can take for truth. Might as well know who and what you're dealing with while he's weak as a newborn kitten." She let the diary drop back onto the table and turned her attention to the kettle simmering over the fire. "We'd best start getting some of this broth down him if you're determined to bring him back from the brink."

After ladling up half a bowl of the soup from the simmering stew, Glory perched on the side of the bed next to the man. "His breathing seems to have eased some," she noted. "Sam Foster, stop that foolishness and come help me get this man sitting up so I can feed him."

Julianne gave the children their stew while Glory and Sam attempted to feed the man. He coughed and muttered incoherently, but did not fully regain consciousness and after three attempts, where most of the broth landed on the buffalo robe, Glory gave up. "I'm sending Sam back to our place to get my things," she announced. "Don't know what I was thinking, leaving you here alone with those children and this stranger."

"We're fine," Julianne protested. "As you said, the man is as weak as a kitten. I'll signal if anything changes," she promised, as Glory launched into a fit of coughing that had Sam looking worried and scared. "Go take care of yourself for once."

"Sam will drive me home and be back before dark. Have young Luke there make a fire near the shed. Sam can bed down out there. And you need to allow him to take his shift watching the patient, while you get some rest." She put on her coat and handed Sam his hat.

Julianne saw her friend's plan for the compromise it was and, in the interest of expediency agreed. She stood in the doorway and waved until the wagon had disappeared into the gray afternoon.

Over the next week, she and Sam took turns sitting with their patient through the night, and Glory kept watch during the day. He'd been in and out of consciousness for over a week, and Julianne was beginning to worry that this might be a repeat of Luke's last days.

"Mama!"

Julianne wheeled around to find the man struggling to throw off the covers and sit up. Both of her children stood close enough for him to grab them if he chose to do so.

"Get back," she ordered as she reached for the hunting rifle Luke had mounted over the door on a rack of moose antlers.

Both children, as well as the man, looked back at her. The children's eyes were wide with surprise at the sight of their mother holding the gun. The man's eyes were red-rimmed and half-closed with fever.

"Stinks," he muttered tearing at the bandages on his chest.

"Stop that right now," Julianne ordered, setting the rifle aside, but within reach, as she positioned herself between the man and her children. "Just stop that and lie back down."

He squinted at her, his thick black hair falling over his eyes, further hampering his vision. "Ah, my angel," he said. And to Julianne's shock, the man laughed.

The sound of it was so unusual in this place where laughter had died with Luke that, for a moment Julianne considered taking the children into the yard and firing the rifle for help. She felt the eyes of her children on her, questioning their next move.

She pointed to their bowls of stew—cold now, no doubt, then wrapped her hands around an iron skillet and eased closer to Nathan Cook. "I'm no angel, mister," she warned. "Try anything and I'll use this."

She brandished the skillet in his direction.

His answer was a soft snore.

Seeing that he'd succeeded in loosening the bandages, and yet reluctant to touch him, Julianne pulled up the buffalo robe and dropped it over him. When Sam returned, she would see to the plaster while he stood guard. In the meantime...

"Mama, what's con-fed-er-ate?" Laura asked, fingering the letter of discharge as she picked at the last of her stew.

Luke had insisted there be no talk of the war, once they'd left all that behind them. But now the war had possibly come to their door, in the form of Captain Nathan Cook.

"There was a war," she explained. "One side was called the Confederate Army and the other was—well, the Federal Army, I guess you could say."

Luke Jr.'s ears perked up. "Did Papa fight?"

"No."

"Why not?" The boy was clearly disappointed.

"It's complicated, Luke, but we decided to move out here."

"Klaus Hammerschmit said that's why they came over here from Germany. There was a war and his father decided to move out here."

"I don't like it when people fight," Laura murmured.

"No, neither do I," Julianne agreed, but she couldn't help glancing back at the man snoring away on her bed and wonder if, before this was all over, she might not have to fight. "Now finish up, and then get to your chores before it gets dark."

While the children scraped out the last of their stew and washed out their bowls, replacing them on the cupboard shelf, ready for their supper, Julianne restacked the papers that had sat on the corner of the table since they'd dried out. Sam had collected them from Nathan Cook's saddlebags and pockets and spread them by the fire to dry that first day they'd found him. She slid the papers back inside the cover of the Bible and placed it inside the saddlebag propped at the foot of the bed. She picked up the diary and paused.

Glory had urged her to read it, but what right did she have? Glory had suggested that the journal might reveal information that could help Julianne decide her course of action, should the man recover.

She fingered the cracked leather cover, then the leather thongs that bound the journal pages. *Just the last few entries*, she decided. Surely that would tell her why he'd come this way and where he was headed. The pages crackled as she pressed the small book open on her lap. She turned to the last entry.

Chapter Two

This land is so different from home. No trees, few streams, and the wind is as relentless as the unending, barren landscape. And then this evening, just as the sun was setting, I stumbled across what back home might have been an orchard of apple or pear trees. It was such a beautiful sight after so many long days of nothing but fields of dead grasses and withered crops, that tears sprang to my eyes. I climbed down from Salt and walked among the low branches and saw the shape of a few hardy leafs undeterred by either the wind or the cold. Oak leaves. I had to smile, then laugh aloud, as I thought of the mighty oak trees that dominate the hills back home.

Julianne glanced at the sleeping man, his breath coming a little easier these last few days. He had been here—right outside. Hers was the only farm in this area that fit the setting he'd described. While she and the children had stayed the night with Sam and Glory, he had passed this way. What if she'd been here? Alone with the children? And yet, he had not broken in. The storm had come on suddenly at dawn, as such things did here on the plains—and passed just as quickly.

As if he felt her watching him, he opened his eyes. "Ma'am?" His voice was raspy.

Julianne started and snapped the journal shut, placing it in her apron pocket.

"Right here," she replied, edging cautiously closer to the bed.

He was lying on his side, and for the first time since Sam had carried him inside his eyes were clear. Only the occasional coughing fit told the story of how very ill he still was.

"Don't want to impose," he managed between coughing jags. "Could I have a little water?"

"Of course," Julianne hurried to the bucket and dipped water into a tin cup. When she turned, he had pushed himself to a position of half-sitting, his weight resting on one forearm.

"Appreciate that," he said when she handed him the cup. His drawl was unmistakable.

"You're Virginian?" she guessed.

He nodded. "How did you know?"

"I grew up there—in the western part of the state."

"Hill country." He grinned and sipped the water. In spite of several day's growth of a thick, black beard, his smile was disarming and at the same time captivating.

"And you?" she asked, forcing her attention anywhere but on those white, even teeth and eyes that were now wide open, and the most startling shade of green—like spring grasses come to life on the plains.

"Just outside Richmond," he managed before the coughing started again. The water sloshed from the cup onto the bedding. "Sorry," he mumbled as he tried ineffectively to clean up the spill.

"Never mind." She took the cup from him. "Are you hungry?"

"Famished," he admitted, "but I don't mean to trouble you—I mean, any more then I already have."

She ignored that and stirred the stew, then ladled up half a bowl and handed it to him.

"What day is it?"

"Monday."

She saw him mentally calculating the lost time. "I've been here a week already?"

"As of yesterday, yes." She handed him the soup and could not help noticing the way he seemed to savor every bite. She would have expected him to gobble it down. After all, it had been days since he'd eaten anything of substance.

"Where are you heading?" she asked.

"California, God willing."

"Well, God seems to have led you straight into the eye of the worst early winter storm we've seen for this time of year." Julianne had little patience with people who placed their lives in God's hands. After all, that's what she'd done with Luke, and he'd died.

Nathan Cook paused with the spoon poised over the

bowl, his eyes searching hers. "God has His reasons for whatever comes our way, ma'am."

It was her turn to shrug. Once a woman of deep, abiding faith, the events of her life over the last few years had convinced Julianne that she could rely on neither man nor God. She had only herself. "We found your papers, Captain Cook. They were quite sodden but we managed to salvage them along with your Bible."

"We?"

"My neighbor and I found you lying in the snow. We brought you here and stabled your horse with the other livestock." She busied herself peeling potatoes to add to the stew.

"May I know your name?"

"I am Mrs. Cooper." Best withhold the fact that she was widowed for as long as possible, Julianne decided.

"And Mr. Cooper?"

"Is not here," she said, satisfied that she had not told an outright lie. "If you'll tell me who to contact, I can see that your family receives word that you are safe."

Julianne was riveted by the expression of abject sadness that briefly shuttered his eyes. "No need," he replied, and turned his face away, whether because of a fresh coughing jag or because he could not bear for her to witness his pain, she could not say.

Just then the door banged in on its hinges, admitting nine-year-old twins engaged in one of their never-ending debates. "I'm telling you that he was on the losing side," Laura insisted. "The papers said that…"

"Children," Julianne interrupted, and the twins stopped in midsentence as they stared past their mother to the stranger smiling at them. "Captain Cook is feeling somewhat better, but still recovering. Please close the door and lower your voices."

Laura did as she was asked while Luke moved closer to Nathan. "Did you fight for the army that won or the one that lost?"

"Luke Cooper, Junior." Julianne knew she did not need to raise her voice. Using the boy's full name never failed to remind him of his manners.

"Sorry," he muttered, and took a sudden interest in looking at the tips of his wet boots.

"Everybody loses in war, son," Nathan said.

It was so close to the answer that Big Luke would have given the boy, that Julianne felt her breath catch, and she was relieved to hear the creak of the wagon wheels on the frozen ground announcing Sam's return. "Go help Mr. Foster unhitch Dusty," she told her son, as she gently guided him toward the door where she could hear another wagon arriving. "Laura, please finish peeling these potatoes while I see who's come calling."

Nathan watched the woman hurry across the room and peek through one of several small holes in the heavily oiled paper that covered the house's only two windows.

"Oh, no," she muttered to herself as she straightened, they pressed her palms over the front of her apron before heading to the door.

Under the spotless bibbed apron made of a calico material, she wore a wool dress of dark gray. It suited her in its simplicity, but seemed exceptionally austere for one so young and vibrant. With her golden hair and pale blue eyes, and cheekbones freckled and kissed by the sun, she was like a ray of sunshine in the otherwise gloomy surroundings.

He saw her glance back at him once she'd recognized her visitors. "Everything will be fine," she assured him in a voice intended to placate and soothe. It was almost as if she expected him to make a run for it.

Within moments, the room was filled with cold air, as well as three women who placed prepared dishes of food on the table. They then surrendered their outer garments to the boy who hung them on pegs. An older black man hung up his hat and coat and stood near the door, as if waiting for the women to settle somewhere.

One of the three—a tall, heavyset woman with a voice that could shatter glass—stood by the door and focused her attention on him as she spoke to the Cooper woman. "I don't know what you could possibly have been thinking, my dear." She clucked her tongue against uneven teeth, and the other two women sidled a little closer to her until they formed what Nathan could only view as a solid line of defense against him.

"You take in a complete stranger, and you all alone here with these dear children?" the woman continued.

"How did you hear of—"

"You were not at services yesterday, and so, naturally, I told Jacob something must be wrong. I thought perhaps the children were ill, or you, yourself. Mind you, the way you insist on living out here alone like this—"

"Sorry," the man by the door said to Julianne. "She came straight to us, and, well…" He shrugged and Julianne nodded.

The older woman ignored this, turning her full attention back to Nathan. "Why have you come here, young man?" she demanded, pointing one stubby finger at him.

"I…" Nathan was not at all sure how to best answer that.

"The man was passed out in the snow," the black man drawled, moving fully into the room now and tapping the bowl of his pipe on the hearth. "There was a choice, that's certain. Leave him where he dropped or take him in."

Nathan was speechless that a black man—an ex-slave by his accent—would speak to a white person with such sarcasm and confidence.

"Just hush, Sam Foster. I am addressing this man here. Well?"

Nathan was thinking a coughing fit might save him, when the Cooper woman stepped forward.

"Captain Cook became disoriented during the storm, Emma," she explained. "He, like so many who have passed our way, is on his way west, to California. Ill as he was, there was little choice but to take him in until he could be moved."

The woman called Emma peered more closely at Nathan. "He certainly won't be going to California until spring—not with an early winter already upon us," she announced. "What's your trade, mister?"

Nathan was speechless at the woman's sudden shift in questioning. "I…"

"The captain served as a chaplain during the war."

All eyes turned to Laura, who was adding onion to the pile of apples and chopped potatoes, as if she hadn't spoken.

"Is that right?" Emma demanded of Julianne.

"According to his papers," she replied.

"Mother, a minister," one of the other two women said, as if this were some sort of good news.

"Hush. And from your accent, may I assume that you are Southern?"

"Virginia, born and bred. Same as Mrs. Cooper here." He had no idea why he'd added that, but it seemed an important point to make.

"Well, I suppose it's true. You had no choice but to do your Christian duty," Mrs. Putnam said, backing away. "Sam, I am assuming that you and Glory will see that Mrs. Cooper—"

"I'm staying in the lean-to for the duration," Sam assured her. "You ladies can rest easy that she and the children won't be alone," he added.

"Very well. But make no mistake, young man," she added, turning her attention back to Nathan, "someone *will* be watching you." She reached for her cloak as the other two women prepared to leave.

"It'll be all right," Sam assured the ladies as he escorted them from the cabin.

Nathan processed this newest bit of information as the women huddled on the stoop, communicating with Sam Foster in urgent and worried whispers. *Where was the husband?* He glanced at the boy and girl—twins by the looks of them. The girl kept casting him curious glances, while the boy edged his way closer to her as if to protect her should Nathan try anything.

Outside, a horse snorted and he heard a wagon pull away, then the black man came back inside with Mrs. Cooper. He folded his arms and studied Nathan while she took the freshly peeled vegetables and added them to a pot over the fire. "Children, it's time for you to work on your spelling," she said, as she put away the bread and cake the women had brought.

"Glad to see you're feeling some better, mister, but just keep in mind that I'm right here," the man the Putnam woman had called Sam Foster warned, as he settled himself in the lone chair close to the door.

"Understood," Nathan said and collapsed back onto the bed, his head spinning. Nothing about these people was making any sense. Neither Mrs. Cooper, whose protector was not her husband but this elderly man, nor the woman from town who had interrogated him and then left. Mrs. Cooper looked as fragile as a china doll, and yet left the definite impression that she could take care of herself. The one thing that he'd heard since regaining consciousness that made any sense at all was the Putnam woman's proclamation that he was going nowhere until spring. He stared up at the makeshift canopy, constructed no doubt to protect the Coopers from bugs and such that might fall from the ceiling of the sod house as he considered his options.

"What is this place?" he asked.

"They named the town Homestead," the girl replied, ignoring her mother's look of warning.

"We're a long way from California," Sam Foster commented, as if making an observation about the weather. "Why are you going there?"

"My brother's there," Nathan replied, not yet ready to give them the whole story.

"Well, there's no hope that you're going to find your way across those mountains before spring—late spring at that." The man lit his pipe and drew on it. "I reckon you could stay with me and Mrs. Foster until you figure out your next move. That would probably be best all around."

"I can work, Mr. Foster," he said, seizing this opportunity God had surely placed before him.

"What'd you say was your trade?"

"I was a chaplain during the war. Before the war my family owned a..." He hesitated to call his family's land by its true name.

"Plantation?" Foster asked.

Nathan nodded.

"Things are different out here," the woman murmured. She glanced at him. "In many ways—not just farming."

"I can see that," he told her, cutting his eyes from her to Foster and back again. "After all I saw these last years, it'd be a nice change."

"You might be thinking about helping out some around here," Sam said. "Those windows could do with some fresh oiled paper if they're expected to keep out the wind and cold this winter."

"I'd be pleased to serve in any way I can," Nathan said. "I'm in your debt, Mrs. Cooper—and yours, Mr. Foster. After all, the two of you saved my life."

"Sam," the older man said. "Just Sam, and my wife's Glory. We'll get you on your feet and then move you over to our place in the next day or so. Let's see how you hold up over the next little bit. No sense in rushing this thing and you having a setback." He sucked on his pipe. "Now, who's gonna help me unhitch that wagon out there?" Both children scrambled to put on their coats and follow him outside.

The silence was suddenly as thick as the smoke-filled air in the close room. The woman picked up some mending.

"May I know your given name?" he asked.

She seemed to consider his request for a long time. "Julianne," she said.

"And your husband's?"

"Luke," she replied, her fingers suddenly still on the fabric. Then she looked up at him, her gaze steady. "My husband died a year ago, Captain Cook."

"I'm so sorry for your loss, ma'am," Nathan said—and he was, but he also couldn't help feeling a certain comfort at the realization that in revealing this information, she had apparently decided to trust him.

Chapter Three

Even after Nathan had been with the Fosters for almost three weeks, it seemed that Julianne Cooper's entire routine had been turned upside down. And she could place the blame for that squarely at the doorstep of one Nathan Cook. The man had a way of being the focus of attention whether he was present or not. Whenever Glory or Sam stopped by, their conversation was about him, and the twins were always curious to know how he was doing. And a parade of townspeople had made it their business to check in on Nathan at the Fosters, and on Julianne, as if they'd suddenly been reminded that she was managing alone now.

On the day that Glory pronounced Nathan well enough to be moved to their farm, Emma Putnam arrived at Julianne's house and, as usual, she was accompanied by her sister, Lucinda, and her daughter, Melanie.

"Good," she announced in her booming voice. "It's high time you got the man out of here, Julianne. It's unseemly for a woman alone—"

"He was too ill," Glory started to protest, but saw the futility of arguing, and pressed her lips together.

"And, Captain Cook," Emma said, turning her attention to him, "you may as well accept that out here on the plains, we don't hold with any social hierarchy. The Fosters are every bit as welcome here and a part of this community as anyone else. I know you're from the South, but—"

"Yes, ma'am," Nathan replied. He leaned heavily on Sam as the older man helped him from the bed and into the wagon. Julianne had followed with the buffalo robe to cover him.

"Oh, no ma'am," he'd protested. "You'll be needing that—you and the children."

"I have another, and Mr. Foster can bring this one back on his next visit," she assured him.

He covered her hand with his, then and peered at her from beneath a fringe of thick, black lashes. "I thank God for bringing me to your home, Miz Cooper."

Julianne had nodded curtly, and slid her hand from between the two of his. She wasn't sure what made her more uncomfortable, the fact that he'd given God the credit for his rescue, or the fact that she could still feel the warmth of his touch radiating through her fingers.

"Come inside this instant, Julianne," Emma called from the doorway, "before you catch your death.

"Captain Cook is quite handsome," Lucinda gushed, once Julianne had returned to the cabin and closed the door.

"Handsome is as handsome does," Emma huffed.

"He's a Southerner, and that's cause for concern. We'll see how he handles himself, now that he's regaining his strength, Lucy—before we make any further assessment of the man's positive attributes."

But whatever reservations Emma Putnam, or anyone else in the community of farmers and townspeople, might have had were erased entirely the first Sunday that Glory pronounced Nathan recovered enough to accompany her and Sam to church. It was the third Sunday of the month, and the circuit preacher was scheduled to hold services in the newly built schoolhouse. The children's desks had all been pushed against the walls and replaced with rows of long wooden benches.

The schoolyard was crowded with wagons and carriages, as farmers and townspeople gathered for the service that was as much an opportunity to socialize as it was to worship. But as the clock over the teacher's desk ticked off the minutes and then an hour, it was apparent that the preacher would not be coming.

"Well," Jacob Putnam said as he stood up and moved to the lectern that served as a pulpit. "Seems we'll have no service today, folks. Shall we—"

"Begging your pardon, sir," Sam Foster said, "but we've a chaplain right here. Perhaps he'd be willing to do a reading and give us a few words before we go?"

All eyes turned to Nathan. He was still gaunt and pale, even after weeks of Glory's cooking, but he stood up, his Bible in his hand. "I could say a few words," he said, looking over the congregation, "if that's agreeable with all?"

There was a general murmur of assent and relief as Nathan made his way to the front of the room. In addition to the usual group that regularly attended services, this was the Sunday before the community's annual harvest homecoming, and the beginning of weeks of preparations for Christmas. The room was so packed with men, women and children that it made the fire in the school's potbelly stove almost unnecessary.

Julianne could not help but notice that Nathan was an impressive figure of a man. He was taller than most of the men in the room, and yet his size was not at all intimidating. In fact, he seemed to exude a kind of confidence and leadership that would naturally draw people to him.

He read a passage from the small Bible that Julianne recognized as the one she'd carefully dried along with his other papers—and his journal. She wished now that she had taken Glory's advice and read more of the journal, and couldn't help wondering what entry he'd made in his journal since leaving her cabin. It shocked her to realize that what she was really wondering was whether or not he might have mentioned her.

After a hymn, Nathan cleared his throat and looked out over the gathering. It was as if everyone had stopped breathing as they waited for the message this Southerner would bring them.

"I had the privilege of meeting young Master Luke Cooper a few weeks ago," he began, and all eyes shifted to where Julianne sat between her two children.

"The boy asked me if I'd been on the winning side

of the war. Now, all of you good people know the outcome of that conflict by now, but I would say to you the
same thing I told Master Cooper. There are no victories
in war—only losses. The loss of sons and husbands
and brothers and fathers—on both sides. The loss of
family ties, as one member chooses one side and another
chooses the other. The loss of homes and farms and
businesses. The loss of unity among states in a nation
founded on unity of purpose. The loss of community.
And far above everything, often there has been the loss
of faith."

Julianne's head shot up. Was it possible that, in their
brief conversation, this man had realized that she had
lost her faith when Luke died? That in standing by help-
lessly as the man who had been her strength and protector faded away day by day, in pain and suffering, with
his children watching, Julianne had questioned a god
who could allow such a thing. And when Luke finally
died, she had not prayed with the others, for she had
spent all of her prayers and all of her tears, and it had
come to nothing. God had not heard her cries for help.

But Nathan was not looking at her as she had expected. He was looking over the crowded room, his eyes
skittering from one upturned face to another. "I am here
to testify that faith can survive even the most horrific
atrocities that man may inflict upon his fellow man. I
am here to say that such faith can not only survive, it
can sustain. Indeed, faith in God is man's only weapon
against despair."

Across the aisle from Julianne, Glory Foster's eyes

brimmed with tears, but she was smiling and nodding and murmuring, "Amen," to each pronouncement out of Nathan's mouth as she clutched Sam's gnarled hand.

"A family is a precious thing," he said, his voice softening. "Every man I ministered to on the battlefield thought first and last of family."

Unconsciously, Julianne placed one hand on Luke's knee and the other on Laura's forearm. *Family. Her family. All she had, now that Luke was gone and her relatives back east had abandoned her because she had defied them to love a Yankee.* She felt her throat close as she thought about the promise she'd made to herself the night that Luke died. His dream—his life—would not have been in vain. She would work the land, maintain the homestead, and protect the legacy that he had wanted for her and their children.

"A community is like family. And although I have only been here a short time, from what I have seen," Nathan continued, "this is a community that has come together to sink its roots deep into the tangled soil of the tall grasses. And now, as you enter this season of harvest and holy days, you have opened your homes and hearts to me—a stranger in your midst and I thank God and each of you for that blessing. Let us pray."

In unison, every head bowed—even Julianne's.

After services, the schoolyard came alive with chatter, as everyone angled for a position to have a word with Nathan. Julianne watched from a distance, waiting for Glory and Sam to have their turn, before she and the children drove to the Foster farm for the noon meal, as they had every Sunday since Luke's death.

She heard Jacob Putnam ask Nathan if he might consider a permanent position as minister of the church the community planned to build in the spring. She moved closer, unsure why his answer seemed so important.

"That's very flattering, sir," Nathan replied. "But California is my destination. My brother is there and he's alone. Like I said before—a man needs to know he has family."

"Contact your brother. Perhaps he might consider—"

"I don't know where he is, sir," Julianne heard Nathan admit then he smiled down at the older man. "But I'd be more than pleased to offer services while I'm here, if that helps."

"It does," Jacob agreed. "And don't think you've heard the last of this. For some in this town, gathering for worship is about as close to family as they're likely to get."

Julianne was sorting through the confusion of her feelings. Shouldn't she feel relief that he planned to move on come spring? Instead, her relief seemed to grow from the news that he would stay for the winter. Why should anything Nathan Cook did concern her in the least?

"Is the captain coming for Sunday dinner?" She heard Luke, Jr. ask as Sam led Glory across the snowpatched schoolyard to their wagon.

"Not today," Glory replied. "Seems Emma Putnam has invited the church elders and the captain to her house."

Julianne had little doubt that her friend was more than a little put out with this affront. "Maybe that's a good thing," she suggested. "It certainly seems as if Emma has had a change of heart when it comes to Nathan—Captain Cook."

Glory glanced over to where Emma was talking excitedly—and loudly—to Nathan, and frowned. "Will you listen to that? All of a sudden she's acting like she wanted to ask him to take the pulpit today all along—like it was her idea, not my Sam's."

"Now Glory," Sam placated.

"She's got her eye on him for other reasons, too. You mark my words, she'll have that scrawny daughter of hers sitting right beside him at the dinner table, but that simpering schoolmarm is no match for that young man. No, sir. He needs a woman who'll stand up to him, walk alongside him—not behind."

Julianne could not help but notice that Glory was looking straight at her as she made these pronouncements.

Throughout the noon meal, all conversation continued to focus on Nathan. Julianne was never so glad to be on her way home. But even, there Nathan Cook's presence filled the tiny cabin.

"Mama?"

Julianne looked up from her needlework to see Laura holding the familiar journal.

"I think this belongs to the captain," Laura said.

"Yes, you're right. It must have slipped out of his saddlebag when he left us. I'll see that he gets it," Julianne promised, taking the book from her daughter.

So there was the answer to her silly, girlish ruminations about whether or not he might have made mention of her in his writings. How could he, when the journal had been here the entire time?

She fanned the pages with her thumb, catching a word here and there. "Jake" was a word she saw more than once as were the words "faith" and "blessed".

The jingle of a harness outside the cabin door made Julianne lay the journal aside as the twins abandoned their game of tiddledywinks and rushed to see who might have come to call. For weeks after Luke died, neighbors had dropped by unannounced several times a day. In some cases, they had been simply curious, clearly half-expecting to find Julianne in the process of packing up for the trip back east. Others had been more direct in their purpose. Emma Putnam came with advice—in her view, Julianne was simply being stubborn and doing her "precious little ones" no favor by refusing to leave.

"It's the captain," Luke, Jr., announced, then threw open the door, bringing in a rush of cold air and a dusting of snow. Nathan ducked to clear the low doorway, removing his hat as he did so. He ruffled Luke's hair and smiled at Laura before turning his attention to Julianne.

"Hello," he said softly, his eyes meeting hers with so steady a gaze that she looked away.

"Well, this is a pleasant surprise," she said, sounding more like Emma Putnam than herself. She picked up the journal. "I expect you've come for this," she continued in a more normal tone. "Laura found it under the bed. It must have fallen out of your saddlebag."

Nathan took it from her and chuckled. "Just goes to show how busy I've been. I didn't even miss it. Writing in it was just a way I used to keep myself company on the trail. But since I moved in with the Fosters, and—what did you think of the service this morning?"

Julianne was taken aback at the sudden change of subject, but Luke rushed in to fill the void. "I was kind of hoping for more stories about the fighting," he said.

"Luke, I believe that you and your sister have chores to attend?"

"Yes, ma'am," the twins replied in unison, as they collected their outer garments and headed for the door.

"Want me to stable your horse?" Luke asked.

"He'll be fine, but thank you anyway."

Luke looked disappointed.

"Come to think of it," Nathan called after him, "Ol' Salt would probably appreciate some water if you could crack the ice on that bucket I saw out there."

"Yes, sir," Luke replied, and ran from the house leaving his sister to make sure the door was closed.

"I apologize," Julianne said when they were gone. "Luke gets his directness from his father."

"And Laura her Southern reticence to pry from you?" Nathan guessed this aloud, as he shifted from one foot to the other. Julianne realized he was still standing just inside the door, still wearing his coat, still holding his hat.

She leapt to her feet and held out her hand for his hat and outer coat. "Well, clearly neither child is learning manners from me today. I'm sorry, Captain, please come and warm yourself by the fire. Even after over three years out here, it's hard to adjust to such bitter cold."

"I was thinking on the way over here how, when I was a kid back in Virginia, at this time of year we were still able to be out in our shirtsleeves." Nathan folded his tall frame onto one of the wooden stools that Luke had fashioned for the table. Luke had been a much smaller man—shorter by a good six inches, and stockier. It was unsettling, seeing Nathan sitting where her husband had once sat.

"Would you like some tea?"

"That would be fine. I'd also really like to know what you thought about today's service."

"Why?"

Nathan smiled. "I thought you said your late husband was the direct one."

"Sorry, but I simply don't know why my opinion should matter one way or another."

"The Fosters have a great respect for you, and that tells me that your opinion has meaning."

Julianne felt the heat rise to her cheeks. "Glory and Sam have been like family to me. I'm afraid they may be prejudiced." She set a mug of tea and a spoon in front of him, and another at her place, then slid the sugar bowl across the table. "Do you take milk?"

"No, thank you." He took a long swallow of the hot liquid, then set the mug down and looked at her. "So?"

"I thought it was fine," she replied.

"Not too much? All that business about us all being pioneers and such?"

"Are you fishing for compliments, Captain Cook?" Julianne laughed, and the sound of it was foreign to her. How long since she had sat at this table and laughed?

Nathan grinned. "Guess I am."

They each drank their tea and Julianne set down her mug and picked up her needlework.

"I'm real sorry for the loss of your husband," Nathan said after a moment. "It must be especially hard this time of year, with Christmas coming and all."

Julianne was so startled that she jabbed herself with the needle and cried out. Nathan reached across the narrow table and examined her finger. "Are you hurt?" He brushed away the single drop of blood with his thumb.

It was the second time the man had taken her hand— the second time she'd been unnerved by the action; and yet, in both cases his attention had been completely innocent and appropriate.

"I'm fine," she assured him. "I often forget to put on my thimble, and I pay the price. Glory says it's because my mind is always on things other than my handiwork," she explained, words coming in a rush, like a creek thawing in spring. "And she may have a point. Certainly, if you look at my work next to Glory's, you'd know at once who paid the attention necessary to get the stitching perfect."

"What other things?"

"What?"

"What are you thinking about when you're stitching?"

The farm. The crops that might never get planted or worse, get washed out if we have a wet spring. The prairie fires that could take everything if we have a dry summer. Having what I need to feed and clothe my children. Making sure that we don't lose this place after all the work that Luke put into it....

Nathan leaned closer and Julianne realized that she had failed to respond to his question. She forced a smile and got up to refill his mug. "Silliness," she said.

"Somehow I doubt that."

"You hardly know me."

"What I know is that it takes a woman of substance to maintain a spread like this, hang onto the only real home her children have ever known. That, and still have the strength to play the Good Samaritan to a stranger stupid enough to try and find his way across the plains with winter coming on."

"How are you feeling?" she asked, relieved at the opening to change the subject.

"Better each day. It's self-defense."

"I don't get your meaning."

Nathan laughed. "Mrs. Foster seems determined to 'fatten me up', as she puts it. She claims I'm skinnier than President Lincoln was, and has this notion that putting food in front of me every couple of hours is the only medicine that can possibly build my strength."

Julianne could not help smiling. "She did the same

thing with me after—" She stopped and covered her mouth with her hand. "Would you like more tea?"

"After your husband died?" Nathan guessed.

Julianne nodded and refilled his cup.

"It will ease—the grief and pain," he assured her.

"I'm sure that on the battlefield you experienced death many times over, Captain. Some of those men were probably friends of yours. And yet—"

"It's not the same," he said, and ran his forefinger around the rim of his cup. "You're right, of course. Still, there are all sorts of losses we must endure over the course of a lifetime. I choose to have faith that each has some purpose."

Her eyes flared with anger. "I fail to see the purpose in leaving those two children fatherless and—"

"I understand how you might feel that way," he said.

She wanted to tell him that he couldn't possibly understand unless he had children who depended on him. But she decided to let the matter drop. After all, he was a guest. "I overheard Jacob Putnam ask you to stay on and consider taking the pulpit permanently."

"Thinking back on it, I suspect it was a compliment, nothing more. I mean, who would hire someone to minister after just one sermon?"

"Jacob takes his role as mayor quite seriously. He's determined to establish Homestead as a viable community as quickly as possible. There's a rumor that the railroad company is looking at a route that could come very close to Homestead."

"Well, I wish him well, and I'm happy to fill in for as long as I'm here, but I have to get to California."

"Your brother?"

Nathan nodded and set his cup on its saucer. "Jake was only sixteen when the war started, but my father thought he was old enough to serve. He couldn't understand why Jake wasn't as eager to volunteer as every other youth in our area."

"But surely your mother—"

"She sides with my father no matter the topic. I was already gone, but apparently the argument escalated to the point where one night Jake just took off. He left a note saying he was headed to California because it was as far away from the war as he could get."

"And you didn't know?"

"I found out when I went home last spring after General Lee surrendered. Mother said they didn't want to tell me, for fear it would upset me and I might get careless. They had lost one son, and they couldn't face losing me as well."

"But Jake wasn't lost."

"He was to them. He had dishonored the family, the South. My father never forgave him—not even on his deathbed. He refused to allow Jake's name to be spoken in that house after the day he left."

"And no one has heard from him?"

"No. As I've traveled west I've placed ads in the California papers, always leaving a general address for a reply, if anyone has seen or heard of him—or if Jake—"

"You don't even know if he's alive?"

Nathan shook his head. "Not for sure. But I have faith that God would not send me off on some wild-goose chase. I believe this is the journey I am meant to be on." He looked up and smiled. "Enough of my misery. What about your family? And your late husband's? Are the twins' grandparents in this area as well?"

"No, my parents are still in Virginia, and Luke's are in Boston." She got up and wrapped her apron around the handle of the kettle. "More?"

The door slammed open and Luke, Jr., burst inside, breathless with the cold and excitement. "The land agent's coming," he announced as Laura crowded in the doorway next to him.

Julianne's hand went to her throat and her eyes widened with alarm as she glanced quickly around the cabin. as if checking to be sure it could stand inspection.

"Is there a problem?" Nathan asked, getting to his feet and moving toward the door.

"No. Maybe." Julianne brushed back a wayward strand of hair. "It's just odd he would come on a Sunday."

Chapter Four

Roger Donner was a large man with a barrel-shaped chest that belied his mild, almost shy manner.

"Afternoon, ma'am," he said, then stopped short when he saw Nathan. "Captain," he added. "Fine sermon this morning."

Nathan extended his hand. "Thank you. I don't believe we had the pleasure of speaking after services."

"Roger Donner, government land agent for the territory." His eyes slid from Nathan to Julianne. "Mrs. Cooper, I wonder if we might have a word…in private?"

Nathan saw Julianne's eyes dart anxiously over the spotless room. "I…this is…" she began.

"It's the Lord's Day, sir," Nathan said quietly. "Surely, any business you have to discuss with Mrs. Cooper can wait until tomorrow?"

"Sadly, no," Donner replied. "I leave first thing tomorrow for St. Louis, to file this year's report with the commissioner for the region." He directed his explanation to Julianne.

Nathan saw Julianne's fingers tighten on her needlework. She jabbed the needle through the cloth and shuddered, and he knew she had once again pricked her finger. "I see," she said softly. "This is about this season's crops, is it?"

"Yes, ma'am. I was in hopes that together we might come up with some way of explaining—"

"My husband died," she said.

"Yes, ma'am. Big Luke was a good man and will be sorely missed." Donner bowed his head even further. "Still, the rules of the Homestead Act are clear. Those living on the land—hoping to claim the land—are responsible."

"Surely there is room for compromise," Nathan said, moving around the table to stand behind Julianne, but resisting the urge to place a comforting hand on her thin shoulder.

Donner shook his head. "No, sir. There's plenty of folks waiting for land—and land with fields already plowed and a house—"

"There's got to be a way 'round it," Nathan said.

"The rules are quite clear, Captain Cook," Julianne said. "If the land lies fallow for a period of six months or more during growing season then it is considered to have been abandoned."

"You could buy it outright," Donner suggested.

"I don't have the two hundred dollars, Mr. Donner."

"I was thinking maybe Mr. Cooper's family back east…"

Julianne stiffened. "That's not possible."

Donner nodded and turned to the door. "Just an idea. I'll do my best, Mrs. Cooper. I wanted to let you know that in person."

"I appreciate that," she said. "How long will you be away?"

"I'll be back in time for Harvest Home," he said brightening a little for the first time since entering the small cabin.

Julianne smiled and pressed his forearm. "Good. We count on you for the music at the festival, you know."

Nathan saw relief flood the man's haggard features, once he realized that he and Julianne seemed to have reverted to their normal friendship. "Yes, ma'am," he said as he left.

"Thank you for riding all the way out here, Mr. Donner. Safe travels," she called, as the man mounted his horse.

"Wait up," Nathan called, taking his hat and coat from the hook where Julianne had hung them. "Mind if I ride along?" He wanted to know more. For starters, why had Donner suggested the dead husband's family and why had Julianne refused so abruptly?

"Not a bit," Donner replied. "Glad of the company."

"I'll stop by later in the week, if that's all right," he said to Julianne, who stood in the yard, her arms wrapped around herself.

"The children and I look forward to it," she replied. "Good afternoon, gentlemen," she called, as the two men rode off together.

Realizing that the way she had been clutching her shoulders had less to do with the weather and more to do with this new bit of worry Donner's visit had brought, Nathan was tempted to turn back to make sure she was all right. But something told him that Julianne Cooper was a woman of pride as well as uncommon strength. She was not likely to appreciate having some stranger see through that pride to the panic and fear he'd seen fill her eyes when Donner had given her his news.

Still, as he and the land agent rode past the fallow fields, snow-covered now, he wondered how any woman alone with two children to raise could possibly live up to the regulations for making the land her own. Acre after acre, the scene was the same—fields clotted with the remains of the last harvest Luke Cooper had gleaned. Roger Donner pointed it all out to him as evidence that he had little choice but to make his report.

"I could lie," he said, "but there's this man who has made a business of buying folks out or reclaiming abandoned land. Miz Cooper's place is one he's had his eye on. It's prime, the way it sits near the river, with its natural supply of water and the way Luke built that soddy so it was protected from the worst of the winter storms."

"She wouldn't want you to lie," Nathan assured the man, and then wondered how he knew that to be true. "God will show her the way," he added. As the two men rode over the uneven and slippery fields, Nathan could only hope that faith was going to be enough.

* * *

Later that evening, Glory Foster told him that after Luke Cooper died, something inside Julianne had hardened. "She sees that those children attend church and all, but I've seen it in her eyes that she's lost faith. And who can blame her—all she's had to endure."

She'd gone on to talk about Julianne's family, who had broken with her when she married Luke—a New Englander—a Yankee. "Then there was his people," Glory continued pursing her lips, as if tasting something bitter. "All kinds of money that family has, but he wanted no part of it if they wouldn't accept Julianne as their equal, even though they had education and all. Big Luke was no more than two months in the ground when she gets this letter from some city lawyer telling her not to try and lay claim to any of the Cooper fortune—as if she would, the way they turned against their own son."

That explained her curt answer when Donner had suggested asking the Coopers for the two hundred dollars she needed to buy the land. With each revelation, Nathan's esteem for the young widow deepened into something that he recognized as more than just empathy for her troubles and admiration for her strength. Was it possible that all along God had been guiding his way, bringing him to this place, that sod house—to her? Julianne Cooper needed help. The problem was that everything about her shouted, *No, I don't.*

Julianne was far more shaken by Roger Donner's visit than she had let on. Standing outside the sod house, she had never felt less suited for the task that she had set for herself.

In the spring after her husband's death, she had hitched their ox, Dusty, to the plow, and set out to prepare the fields that surrounded their cabin for planting. But she had made it barely half a row before blisters had formed on her palms and her skirts and boots were coated with mud. She'd looked up then and seen a man astride a large white steed, watching her from the top of the rise.

Two days later the man had come calling and suggested that going it alone was not the answer. If she would allow him to assume ownership of her land…

She'd lost her temper and ordered him off her property. But the man had not given up. He had only changed tactics. Instead of trying to buy her out, he had tried courting her. He would stop by on the pretense of bringing Laura a book he'd seen when the peddler came through town. He offered Luke, Jr., his pocketknife. Julianne had quietly refused every gift, and eventually he stopped coming. But he was out there. She'd heard of a man of his description traveling the region, reclaiming abandoned homesteads and buying out those who found the winters too severe and the summers too hot.

Later that week, as she peeled apples for apple butter and counted the days until Roger would return with news of her fate, she felt the familiar weight of responsibility settle round her shoulders. The rules of the contract were simple—either manage the land or lose it. Even though her neighbors had offered to put in crops for her, she'd been too proud to accept charity. Besides, Roger had made it clear that eventually she would have to find a way to work the land herself.

"Mama, you're cutting too close to the core," Laura reprimanded, as she picked an apple seed out of the bowl and laid it on the table.

Julianne stared at the tiny black seed, her paring knife suspended in midair, the seed reminding her of the thousands of seeds it would take to plant her fields come spring.

The shroud of hopelessness that covered her made her knees shake, and she sank down onto a kitchen stool.

"Mama?"

Laura was peering at her. "Are you sick? Should Luke go for Miz Foster?"

"I'm fine," she assured both children. "We're fine," she added through teeth gritted in determination that she would not fail them.

Ever since President Lincoln had called for a national day of thanksgiving, towns and villages across the land had held prayer services and festivals in observance. The date varied from one community to the next, but the celebration found its framework around faith and food and friendship. Homestead's festival was scheduled for the last weekend in November.

The day of the festival, Julianne braided Laura's hair and ironed a shirt for Luke. She took more time than usual with her own hair and clothing. Ordinarily, she would have chosen the black dress she had worn for Luke's funeral and to every public gathering since. But the anniversary of Luke's death had passed quietly that week, with only Glory taking note. "Time to move on," she'd advised. "Luke would have wanted that for you."

And so she chose her best dress, a woollen homespun the color of pine trees back in Virginia. She braided her hair and then wrapped the long braids around her head in a coronet, fastening them in place with the pair of silver combs Luke had given her as a wedding present.

"You look pretty, Ma," Laura said.

"Yeah—different, but real pretty," Luke added.

"Thank you. Now get your coats and mittens on. Mr. and Mrs. Foster will be here soon and we don't want to be late."

The Putnam barn had been transformed for the festival. Bales of fresh hay did double duty as decoration and seating. Piles of pumpkins, squash and gourds filled freshly swept stalls—the animals having been moved to neighboring farms for the occasion. Dozens of lanterns swung from rafters and cast a warm glow over the festivities below.

In one corner, the children were gathered around their teacher in her new role as organizer of games and contests for the evening. A barrel filled with melted snow and apples waited for the children to try and snag an apple without using their hands. Across the way, Roger Donner and a trio of farmhands were warming up their fiddles in preparation for a sing-along and dancing. Roger had avoided Julianne since she and the children had arrived, and that more than anything told her that he had likely failed to successfully plead her case with the commission.

"Come along, Julianne," Emma bellowed. "The contest is about to begin." She took Julianne by the arm and steered her to the end of a long bench that had been placed in the center of the barn.

Julianne unwrapped her paring knife from the napkin she used to protect its sharp blade, and sat on the edge of the bench. Lucinda Putnam moved up and down the rows, handing each woman an apple.

"Now, ladies, you have one minute to produce the longest unbroken strand of apple peel," Jacob Putnam instructed, taking out his pocket watch and flicking open the cover. "Ready, set, go."

In seconds, several of the younger and less experienced women were eliminated as the peels of their apples broke. Soon it was down to Julianne and two others. She considered allowing the streamer of peel to break of its own weight, giving one of the others a better chance at the victory, but then she caught Nathan watching her closely.

He smiled and nodded, and she found herself wanting to please him. She narrowed her cut a sixteenth of an inch, to give herself the best chance at having the longest strand.

"Time," the banker called, as Lucinda carefully gathered the peels created by the three finalists and took them off for measurement. "And while we await the outcome," Putnam shouted, "we shall ask the single ladies to take their places and peel one more apple."

There were giggles and excited whispers, as girls and single women took their places on the benches. Julianne started to get up, but Glory placed a firm hand on her shoulder and handed her an apple.

"Let's just see if there's a new man in your future, missy," she said.

"Don't be ridiculous."

"Peel," Glory ordered as, one by one, the others peeled their apple and tossed the skin over their shoulder. Then everyone gathered to see what initial the peel might have formed, for legend had it that the peel would form the letter of a girl's intended.

"Well, look at that. Is that the letter C, or could it be the letter N?" Emma boomed as everyone gathered around.

"I think it's more of a J," someone suggested. "Is it supposed to be the first or last name?"

"First," someone replied.

"Well, now that I study it, that's an N as clear as writing it on the chalkboard," Emma insisted.

"The letters C and N don't look nothing alike," someone shouted, and others murmured their agreement as Emma defended her position.

"Drop yours while they're busy chewing on that," Glory instructed.

"Glory," Julianne protested.

"Just humor an old woman and drop the peel."

Julianne refused to toss the peel over her shoulder as tradition dictated. Instead, she dropped it on the floor in front of Glory, and there was not a doubt in the world that the letter the red apple skin most resembled was an N.

"Told you so," Glory said, scooping up the peel before anyone else could see it and walking off toward where the children were bobbing for apples.

Julianne continued to stare at the dirt floor where the peel had lain. She did not believe in such silliness, but on the other hand, the moisture from the peel had left its imprint, and she could not deny that it formed the first letter of Nathan's name.

It had been a year, and in all that time the idea that she might find love again had been the furthermost thing from her mind. And yet...

"And the winner and new champion of the apple-peeling contest with a ribbon of twenty-three inches is," Putnam shouted, "Mrs. Julianne Cooper."

A cheer went up as Julianne stepped forward to receive her prize, an apron embroidered with apples on the pocket.

"Thank you," she said.

"Louder," someone called.

"Thank you," she shouted, and everyone laughed. "But let us all remember that the champion will always be Mrs. Foster, until her record can be broken."

"And now, ladies and gentlemen, boys and girls, it's time for the judging of the baked goods," Jacob announced. "Captain, will you do the honors?"

The crowd followed Nathan over to where the cakes, pies and sweetbreads were displayed.

She watched as he tasted one sweet after another and announced that choosing the best was an impossible task. In the end, he declared a tie between Emma's pumpkin pie and Glory's apple cake.

"That was very nice of you," she told him later, as they sipped glasses of apple juice and watched the children engaged in a lively game of blindman's buff. "Everyone knows that Emma Putnam has many skills, but baking isn't one of them."

He shrugged. "Some people need that recognition, and it costs nothing to give it to them now and again."

"So you admit it," she pressed.

He grinned. "Between you and me? Yes."

"Why, Reverend Captain Cook, I am shocked." His laughter carried above the squeals of the children, warming the air around them.

"It's getting so close in here, and the night is clear. Would you walk with me, Julianne?"

Outside, several men had gathered around a fire to talk in peace and smoke their pipes as couples strolled hand in hand under the star-filled sky.

"I see Roger Donner is back," he said.

"Yes."

"And?"

"We haven't spoken, but I know that's the answer. If he'd been successful in getting me more time he would have told me right away. He wants me to have this evening to enjoy. He's a good man."

"What will you do?"

"I don't know," she admitted.

He pulled her hand through the crook of his elbow. "We'll figure something out," he said. "Meanwhile, Roger has a good idea. Let's just enjoy this evening."

They walked along in silence until they came to a rail fence, the silence stretching uncomfortably between them. "I hate seeing you so sad," he said finally.

"Not sad so much as..." She searched for the right word. "That is, I was very sad for a long time after Luke became so ill and died."

"Only sad?"

"And angry," she admitted.

"At God?"

"I'm afraid I don't have your strength when it comes to faith," she said. "Yes, I was angry at God—and at Luke."

"For dying?"

"For leaving me and the children, I suppose. Oh, I know that he didn't choose that path—no one does. But life can be so very hard sometimes. Don't you ever feel that?"

He stared out at the horizon for a long moment, and she wondered if he was thinking about his lost brother.

"I'm sorry," she said, touching his shoulder to draw his attention away from the past. "Glory says I spend too much time dwelling on things I can't change." She was struggling to lighten the mood, to bring them back to the place where he was laughing and his laughter made her feel light as air.

"Glory is a wise woman," he said, cupping her cheek with his palm.

In that moment it was as if the world had stopped turning and they were alone in the dark with only the endless horizon and a sky filled with stars surrounding them.

"Julianne," he whispered as he lowered his mouth to hers. And any idea that she had that he might have been mourning his missing brother flew away on the wings of his kiss.

His lips were soft and met hers gently, tentatively, and even when she returned his kiss, he did nothing to take advantage. Instead, he pulled away and rested his forehead on hers. "You could always come to California," he whispered. "You and the children."

Panic laced with confusion threatened to overwhelm her. Her knees shook and she grasped the fence railing for support as she stepped away from him. "How can you think that problems can be so easily solved?" she managed to say.

"I don't. I just…" He reached out to touch her and she backed away.

"I can't leave here," she told him.

"Why not? Think of it, Julianne. A fresh start. California is filled with possibilities."

"You don't know that. You've been taken in by what

you've read and heard and you have a purpose in going there. Your brother..."

Now he was the one who took a step back. "And what is your purpose in staying here?"

"I promised," she said, choking a little on the words as she realized that already she had broken that promise, because she had most likely lost the land. She was suddenly aware of music coming from the barn, lively and incongruous to the tension between them. "I have to go," she said. "I need to speak to Roger—to know for certain...."

She did not finish her statement, and as she ran back toward the light of the barn, she realized that she felt only disappointment that Nathan did not try to stop her.

Chapter Five

Roger tried to persuade her that there was still hope in that the commissioner had postponed making any decision until after Christmas, but Julianne saw in the land agent's eyes that he did not believe the decision would be in her favor.

She didn't take the children to church on Sunday. Luke had the sniffles, and while she knew it wasn't serious, that was her excuse. On Monday she found herself listening for the creak of Sam's old wagon, knowing if it came it would most likely be Nathan driving the team.

But Nathan did not come. Glory stopped by to check on the children but remained uncustomarily silent regarding Nathan. A week passed, and an unexpected snowstorm gave Julianne the only excuse she needed to miss church for the second week in a row.

Late on Monday night, after the children had been in bed for an hour already, Julianne heard the pound of hoofbeats coming down her lane. She wiped her hands on her apron and waited for the rider to pass, but the only sound she heard was the relentless wind that whistled around the house seeking any possible entry, and the low murmur of a man's voice instructing his horse. Then boots, heavy on the stoop outside her door, followed by a light tap.

She glanced at the rifle over the door, then at the lamp she'd left burning while she finished putting up the last of the apple butter that she hoped to trade at the mercantile for toys for the twins' Christmas.

"Julianne?"

The voice was muffled and indistinguishable. Not Sam Foster. But who else might call at this late hour?

"Who's there," she said, standing very close to the door so that there was no need to raise her voice and risk waking the children.

"It's me—Nathan. Look, I know it's late but..." When she failed to answer or open the door, he knocked again louder. "Julianne, please. I need to talk to you."

She grabbed her wool shawl and wrapped it around her head and shoulders, then slipped outside. "The children are sleeping, Captain Cook," she said. "Has something happened to Sam or Glory?"

"Not at all," he assured her. "They're both fine."

"Then why—"

"Walk with me a minute," he urged, taking her elbow.

It was absolutely foolhardy to do as he asked. And yet, even as she took in the restless stirring of the animals in the lean-to and saw that it was a clear night with a sky filled with stars, she did not pull away.

"Captain, really," she protested, but she followed his lead until they were standing in the midst of the apple trees that she and Luke had planted shortly after the house had been completed.

Nathan bent and scraped away snow until he unearthed a fallen apple. "This," he said holding the rotted fruit up as if it were gold, "could be your answer."

"It's an apple," she said slowly, as she might have years earlier when she was teaching the twins to identify objects.

"And how was this year's crop?" he asked, putting an unusual emphasis on the last word.

"It was really the first," she explained. "Luke and I planted the saplings three years ago when we first arrived here. It takes some time for—"

"I know. So how was the crop?"

Again that unusual focus on "crop".

"Captain—"

"Nathan," he corrected.

"Nathan, it is late. It is freezing. And my children are sleeping. What do you want?"

"You harvested these apples—what you could, right?"

She nodded impatiently.

"You probably dried some, put up some butter, perhaps made a pie?"

"Three," she corrected. "In fact, as long as you're

here you can carry one back with you for the Fosters."
She turned and started back around the house.

But once again he stopped her, his hand taking her
forearm and turning her so that she was facing the apple
trees and he was standing behind her with his hands
resting lightly on her shoulders. "Think of it, Julianne,"
he said. "Imagine not just these few saplings, but apple
trees as far as you can see."

She had lost most of the feeling in her hands and feet,
and yet there was a warmth emanating from him that
held her where she stood.

"Think of spring and white and pink blossoms everywhere you look, like clouds come down to earth," he
said, his voice soft, dreamy. "Think of the blossoms
falling like snow, and then the apples coming, green at
first, and then brilliant yellow and red, like maple trees
back home in Virginia come autumn."

The picture he painted was mesmerizing. She forgot
about the cold, forgot about the late hour. "An orchard,"
she murmured.

"A crop," he corrected. "A legitimate use of the land
and one you have already begun. You didn't abandon
the land, Julianne. Right here there was a crop."

She turned to face him. "Do you honestly think the
commissioner would accept that?"

"I spoke with Roger after I remembered seeing these
apple trees the day before the storm came up so sudden,
and I got disoriented. I mentioned the idea to Roger and
he sent off a letter to the commissioner that very day."

"But Roger said that the best he could do was get a decision postponed until after the first of the year."

"And it may be weeks before you have an official answer. But Roger agrees with me as does Judge Romney." He pulled a paper from his jacket pocket. "This is a copy of the law, and it says right here that you've met the requirements—you raised a crop. You raised and harvested apples."

"It's a few fruit trees," she protested, afraid to let herself surrender to the hope he offered.

"There's nothing in the regulations to specify the size of the crop, Julianne. Roger agrees. It's the intent to farm the land that counts, and these trees show intent."

She felt the way a bird that had just experienced flight for the first time must feel. Weightless. Free. Without thinking, she flung her arms around Nathan's neck. "Oh, Nathan, thank you. It's brilliant. It's…"

She felt his arms tighten around her, his breath against her cheek as he bent his face to hers. Reality hit like a sudden drop in temperature. She reminded herself of the hour, the isolation, the compromising circumstances of being in each other's arms.

"It's freezing out here," she said abruptly, releasing him and stepping back as she clutched the shawl more tightly around her. "Come warm yourself by the stove for a bit before you head back."

She stumbled over the uneven and frozen ground until she reached the front door. Inside, she went first to check on the children, lifting the curtain that surrounded their cots to assure herself that they were both still asleep. She was aware that he had followed her inside and closed the front door.

Without meeting his gaze, she hurried over to the stove and lifted the kettle. "I'll just…"

His hand on her shoulder made her go still.

"Sit down and warm yourself," he said, relieving her of the kettle. "I'll do that."

Gratefully, she did as he instructed, pulling the stool nearer to the fire and holding out her hands to the embers.

He handed her a cup of tea and she wrapped her palms around the warm crockery. Nathan knelt next to her and before she could protest, he had pulled off her shoes and set them on the hearth to dry. Then he wrapped his thick knitted scarf around her feet.

"Better?" he asked looking up at her.

She nodded, unable to find her voice. Unable to decipher the feelings racing through her brain as she looked at him.

"Now then," he said, taking the bench across from her, "you still have to come up with a plan for planting more trees, building the crop. There's still work to be done."

She tried to focus on what he was saying, but could get no further than remembering the feel of his gentle touch as he swathed her feet in the soft wool of his scarf. He picked up an apple seed that had stuck to the table. "You'll need seeds and—"

"But until we know for certain…" she said, reminded of how Luke had rallied for a few days and then slipped away. She had to stop daydreaming and focus on the hard realities of what lay ahead for her and the children.

"You know. You have it right there in writing," he said, nodding toward the copy of the law he'd given her.

She bent and unwrapped her feet, then folded the scarf in thirds and handed it to him. "Then we'll be fine. Thank you so much, Nathan. You didn't have to—"

"I could help you work out the plan for the planting, order the seeds."

In the days since he'd kissed her she had a lot of time to think, and the one thing she knew was that it would be foolhardy to get any more involved with this man than she already was. Every act of kindness bound her more closely to him and would make his leaving all the more painful. She stood up. "As I said, I am so very grateful for all that you—and Roger—have done for us. We'll be fine now—the children and I."

He stood as well. Slowly, he wrapped the scarf around his neck. "There's an old adage," he said quietly, "that God helps those—"

"What would you have me do?" Her voice was tight and rising. With a glance toward the curtain sheltering her sleeping children, she lowered it to a whisper. "I cannot plant trees when the ground is frozen."

Nathan started to say something, but instead turned and walked the three steps it took to reach the door. His silence made Julianne feel guiltier than if he had argued with her. After all he had come up with this idea—this plan that might make keeping her promise to Luke possible.

"Thank you for coming—for trying to help—for…" Her voice broke then, so that the last word came out on a sob. "…caring."

Nathan turned and pulled her hard against him, holding her as she cried.

"You aren't alone," he whispered. "There are so many people who want to see you succeed. Don't shut them out, Julianne."

She forced a laugh and pulled away, determined to show him that she was fine. "How is it that with everything you've been through, you are so sure things will work out for the best?"

He smiled and pushed a wayward curl behind her ear. "I'll answer that when you tell me how it is that you are so very sure that they won't." He pulled his hat on, anchoring it firmly over his brow. "Goodnight, Julianne."

Chapter Six

In spite of the way she'd tried to refuse his help that night, Nathan made a habit of stopping by every day the following week. In answer to her look of exasperation, he would turn his attention to the children. He would help with the chores and sometimes agree to stay for supper when one or both of the children suggested he should.

While Laura helped Julianne with the housework, Nathan and Luke tended to the evening chores. Through the hole-pocked paper that covered the windows, Julianne could hear the low murmur of Nathan's conversation with her son, although she could not make out the topic. Lately, many of the sentences out of young Luke's mouth seemed to begin with, "The captain says…"

Luke's sudden shriek brought her to the door at a run. Outside, she saw Nathan standing near the lean-to, and he was grinning at Luke who was trying in vain to brush fresh snow off his hair and neck. "Well?" Nathan challenged with a grin.

Luke scooped up a lump of snow and slowly formed it into a ball as he advanced on the preacher.

"Luke, no!" Julianne protested, just as the snowball found its mark smack in the middle of Nathan's chest.

"Good one," Nathan said, even as he grabbed another handful of snow and flung it back at Luke.

The battle was on in earnest now, and before Julianne knew what was happening, Laura squeezed past her, having donned her coat and mittens, and joined her brother in the fray.

"Ganging up on me, are you?" Nathan called, as he ducked a lob from Laura. "Mrs. Cooper, I need reinforcements," he called.

As if she'd traveled back in time to when she was younger, still living in the hill country of Virginia and unencumbered by responsibility, Julianne scooped some snow from the porch and flung it at her children.

"Ma!" Luke protested, but he was laughing and so was Laura, and the sound shattered the last dregs of somberness that had surrounded their home for far too long. Luke was gone, but she had her children. And when Julianne heard her own laughter in chorus with theirs, it was like music in the cold December air, and she felt that somewhere in the heavens above, Luke was laughing with them.

By the time supper was ready, any trace of uneasiness or shyness that might have dampened the meal had been banished by the snowball fight. As they bowed their heads for Laura to offer grace, Julianne could not help but notice that, for the first time in nearly a year, gathering for a meal together felt truly special. And she owed that—like so many changes that had taken place over the last several weeks—to Nathan Cook.

"Thank you, God, for this food we are about to receive," Laura prayed. Assuming his sister's prayer would begin and end as their grace always did, Luke's hand shot out to retrieve the first of the biscuits. But Laura scowled at him from under lowered lashes and continued. "And thank you for sending Captain Cook to us. And thank you for making Mama so happy today. Amen."

"Amen," Nathan added, looking across the table at Julianne.

"Luke, please pass our guest the biscuits first before you serve yourself," she instructed, glad for the excuse of teaching a lesson in manners to avoid meeting Nathan's questioning gaze. The man had to be wondering why her happiness was so unusual as to be a part of the blessing of the food.

"Captain Cook," Luke said, his voice breaking slightly with nervousness. "I know you said nobody wins at war, but can I ask you something else?"

"Yes."

"Did you carry a gun?"

"Yes."

"Then you know how to use a rifle like my Pa's?" Luke glanced at the rifle mounted over the door.

Julianne knew exactly where this was going. Luke's father had promised to teach the boy to fire the rifle and to take him hunting this fall. He'd filled the boy's head with tales of how they would shoot a wild turkey and bring it home for a feast at Christmas. "Luke, this is hardly—"

"I can do that," Nathan replied at the same moment. He looked to Julianne for guidance before continuing. "Tell you what, Mr. Foster and I were talking about doing some hunting. Glory has her heart set on a wild turkey for Christmas dinner. With the snow on the ground, tracking comes easier."

"Yes, sir," Luke said, his eyes sparkling with hope.

"If your mother agrees, Mr. Foster and I could let you come along, help with the tracking."

"Could I, Mom?"

On the one hand, Julianne felt cornered. On the other, she was well aware that this day had to come. And Nathan was offering her son a safe entry into the man's world of hunting.

Taking her hesitation as a good sign, Luke pressed his case. "I'll do all my chores without you having to ask, and I'll practice my multiplication tables and—"

"I suppose, if Mr. Foster is willing. But you'll do no shooting," she said.

Luke started to protest, but Nathan gave the boy a signal that had him agreeing to her terms. "Then I can go?"

"Yes, but on one condition."

His smile wavered.

"I want to hear you recite your multiplication tables all the way to twelve times twelve without looking to your sister for hints," she said. "The day you can do that is the day you can tell Captain Cook here that you are ready to go hunting."

Luke's face fell. Math was not his strong suit.

"I'll help," Laura said softly. "Come on, Luke, it'll be fun. Like playing school."

Luke groaned and Julianne could not hide her grin. Laura's favorite game was "school". She would line up her two dolls and teach them the lessons she'd learned that week. She would also beg Luke to play along, but he usually refused. A chance to make both of her children so happy was not something Julianne was going to pass up.

"I think that's a fine idea, Luke," she said.

"Yes, ma'am," Luke said, admitting defeat. "But once I can say the tables, I don't have to play any more?"

"Seems to me that playing school with your sister every now and again might not be such a bad thing," Nathan said. "Seems to me there might even come a time when you'd play the part of the teacher—maybe teach her about tracking," he suggested.

"Yes," Luke exclaimed, his high spirits restored.

"I should be heading back," Nathan said, as he pushed his plate away and wiped his mouth on his napkin. "I was thinking that tomorrow we might get you a tree to decorate for Christmas."

"Oh, that would be wonderful," Laura squealed. "Last year—" She glanced at Julianne and went silent.

"Last year," Julianne explained, "we didn't really celebrate Christmas. The children's father had recently died, and—"

"Then all the more reason to celebrate twice as much this year," Nathan said, addressing himself to the children. "I expect the two of you have already started on your gifts, right?"

Both children looked blank.

Nathan sighed. "I can see I'm going to have to take charge here—show you folks what an old-fashioned Virginia Christmas looks like."

Julianne was overwhelmed by the sudden need to keep her hands and thoughts busy with something other than the way Nathan looked, sitting opposite her and laughing with her children.

Like he belongs, she thought.

Early the following morning Nathan returned.

"Captain's back," Luke announced excitedly as he ran to the door.

"Good morning," Nathan called out when Julianne and the children came out onto the narrow porch. "Ready to go fetch that tree?"

As usual, the man was in fine spirits. There was something so appealing about that, and she found herself wishing she could find that kind of peace and contentment with life. She realized that she envied him this.

"Good morning," she replied as Luke bolted from her and peered curiously into the back of the wagon.

"What's that?" the boy asked.

"What's that, *sir*," Julianne corrected automatically, her own curiosity piqued.

"Sir," Luke added.

Nathan lifted two flat packages, each wrapped in brown paper and string. "Glass panes for the windows," he explained. "Careful now," he instructed, as he handed Luke one of the packages.

"I can take the second one, sir," Laura volunteered.

"And I thank you for that. Leaves me free to gather these tools," Nathan told the girl.

The twins carried the packages onto the porch as if they were precious gold, and set them carefully on the table that in warmer weather held the pitcher and bowl for washing up.

"I don't understand," Julianne said. "I didn't place an order for glass panes with Mr. Putnam, and this is a sod house, captain."

"I placed the order," Nathan said with a grin. "See, I was thinking that if you had glass in the window openings, then you could start some apple seeds inside—plant them in tin cans there on the window ledge. The sun through the glass would be warmer—like spring, and by spring you'd have a seedling instead of just a seed."

"I really…" She could barely find the words to form the protest.

"Have a little faith, Julianne," he said softly.

Julianne wrestled with her irritation that he would assume she had money for such things. "I cannot…"

Nathan moved a step closer and lowered his voice, his eyes on the children busily unwrapping the precious glass. "You cannot what, Julianne? Afford? Accept?"

"Both."

"It's a gift. My thanks for the care you gave me. I might have died had you not taken me in. Seems to me that a couple of panes of glass is hardly repayment enough for saving a man's life." He gave her a moment to consider his argument. "Please accept this, Julianne."

"Your thanks were enough," she murmured, but her eyes were on the glass pane that Laura was holding up to the light. Glass in the window wells instead of the oiled paper would do far more than help her raise apple seedlings. It would block out the wind and cold. It would allow more light into the cabin—into the lives of her children. "Very well," she said. "I accept, and now it is I who am in your debt."

Nathan laughed. "If you look at it that way, we could play this round-robin of thank-you gifts for years to come, Julianne."

His good humor was contagious, and Julianne smiled up at him. "Would that be so terrible?" It was the kind of flirtatious comment she might have made to Luke in their courting days. She felt the heat rise in her cheeks.

His smile faded and his eyes softened. "Not bad at all," he murmured, then cleared his throat and turned his attention to the children. "What do you say, children? If we work together we can have these panes in place and sealed by noon, and *then* go cut that Christmas tree."

She watched him instructing the children with patience and confidence in their ability to do as he asked. From time to time he would glance her way, as if they shared some bond built around their love of children. And she realized that for the first time since Luke's death, the idea that she might one day marry again was not as far-fetched as she had once thought.

But it could not be Nathan, she thought sadly. She would not keep him from following his dream of reuniting with his only brother and making a fresh start in California. But she would never forget the man who had opened the window to the possibility that she would not fail.

True to his word, the windows were fully installed by noon, and light seemed to pour into the cabin.

"Mama, look," Laura said, "I can see well enough to do my schoolwork here by the window."

"We'll have to make curtains," Julianne replied. "I think I have just the fabric." She rummaged through her sewing basket and pulled out two pieces of calico. "What do you think?"

"I think," Nathan announced, "that if we don't get going we'll not find a tree for Christmas before dark."

She spun around, unaware that Nathan had come inside.

"Oh, you and the children go on," she said.

He frowned. "Choosing and cutting the tree is a family thing, Julianne. Come with us." He took her cloak from the hook and held it out to her.

A family thing, she thought, and wished it might be so.

Chapter Seven

Nathan watched Julianne herd the twins into the back of the wagon bed mounted on runners. She was such a small woman—not more than five feet in height—and yet she carried herself with such strength and determination. He'd have to take care in the way he offered his advice—about the orchard or anything else—for she was also a proud woman. He suspected that underneath that brave front lay the kind of fear that he'd seen more than once on the battlefield. What if an officer could not spare his men from the ravages of the battle they were about to fight? What if that officer made a mistake and chose a path that would lead not to victory but to utter defeat?

"Ready?" he called over his shoulder to the children.

"Ready," they chorused, and then laughed with sheer delight as Nathan snapped the reins and the team took off at a trot across the snowy fields.

Back in Virginia, the challenge of a hunt for the tree

was choosing the best one. Here, the problem was finding a tree—any tree. He suspected that Julianne was well aware of his dilemma when he saw her cover her mouth with one gloved hand and pretend an intense interest in the monotonous scenery that surrounded them.

"Not exactly Christmas-tree country," he muttered, and heard her gulp back a giggle. "You might have warned me."

"The first Christmas Luke and I spent here, we searched for hours."

"And found?"

She laughed. "A little scrubby evergreen that we decorated with a single paper star and a strand of ribbon. It was so tiny, that's all it would hold."

The twins were beginning to bicker over shares of the buffalo robe in the back of the wagon. "Are we there yet?" Luke demanded with an exasperated huff. "I'm freezing."

"You're cold," Julianne corrected, "not freezing. And no, we have not seen a tree yet."

"We're not giving up, are we?" Laura asked, and Julianne realized how important this Christmas was going to be for her children. It marked a return to normal, an end to mourning.

"Tell you what," Nathan announced, "let's make a game of the hunt. First one to spot a proper tree wins the prize."

"What's the prize?" the twins chorused.

"Well now, let's see. If Laura wins, then she gets a

yard of ribbon from the mercantile. If Luke wins, he gets a nickel's worth of penny candy."

"What about Mama?" Laura asked.

Nathan glanced at Julianne's cheeks, as rosy as a ripe apple. "Apple seeds," he said softly, "for her orchard."

Their eyes met, and for an instant he held her gaze before focusing on her lips.

"Not fair," Luke declared.

"Fair if I'm making the rules," Nathan countered. "When you come up with a game—and the prizes—then you get to set the rules."

He sounded like a father—not *his* father certainly, but the father he and Jake had always wished they might know. How Jake would laugh if he could hear Nathan now.

"Trees," the twins screamed in unison, pointing to a cluster of juniper trees in the distance.

"I win," Luke crowed.

"I saw them, too," Laura protested.

"It's a tie," Julianne said, quieting both children as Nathan snapped the reins and the team of horses trotted across the barren landscape toward the trees.

"Not exactly a forest," Nathan said with a grin.

"It seems a shame to cut even one," Julianne said. "Trees are so very scarce out here."

"Aw, Ma, it's Christmas," Luke groaned, kicking at a branch that had broken off one of the trees.

Nathan bent and picked up the branch, oddly shaped but still green with needles. Then Julianne pulled another small branch from the snow.

"If we tied them together," she said, "they'd almost have the right shape."

Nathan handed her his branch and watched as she arranged the two so that one's greenery covered the other's bare spots.

"Here's another," Laura called, running to collect a smaller branch. "If we find enough we could build our own tree."

The search was on.

"No fair breaking branches off, Luke," Laura instructed.

"Now who's making up the rules," Luke muttered, but released the branch he'd been trying to break off one of the live trees.

The four of them had soon collected enough greenery to make an impressive tree and then some. "This is fun," Luke shouted as he added another branch to the pile in the back of the wagon.

"No doubt about it," Nathan said, "you two found us a treasure when you spotted this grove."

"We've enough to make a tree for our cabin and one for the Fosters as well." Julianne was beaming. "It will be a wonderful surprise."

"Come on," Luke urged. "Let's get home so we can build the trees."

Everyone piled into the sled and the horses started for home. The scent of juniper berries surrounded them and Nathan could not remember the last time he had felt such anticipation for Christmas to come.

"You know, when Jake and I were just boys," he said, "we used to go into the woods looking for mistletoe. It grew in the tallest trees, and Pa would shoot it down."

"My father did that as well," Julianne remembered. "I always begged him to let me go along, but he said it was a man's job." She got a faraway look in her eyes and frowned. "He was very rigid about such things."

"Sounds like my father," Nathan admitted. "Jake and I always said that if we were ever lucky enough to marry and have kids of our own, things would be different."

"You'd make a wonderful father, Nathan."

It was a simple compliment, and yet the words warmed him as if he'd just downed a steaming cup of hot chocolate.

"Wonder if Jake's a father yet," he mused, embarrassed at the effect her words had had on him.

"You've had no word at all?"

Nathan shook his head. "I keep hoping, and now that I'm to be in Homestead over the winter, I've sent out ads and letters to every community I can think of between here and California. It occurred to me that maybe he stopped along the way and stayed."

"He could be closer than you imagine." Julianne placed her gloved hand on his forearm. "You mustn't give up hope."

But she *had*, Nathan thought. According to Glory, after her husband's death she had locked her heart away.

The jingle of the harness brought Nathan back to the present. The cabin was in sight, the afternoon sun glinting off the newly installed window panes, as a stream of smoke wafted from the chimney and seemed to signal "home" as it dissipated against the overcast sky.

In spite of her resolve not to become more involved with the man, Julianne could think of nothing but Nathan. As she did her morning chores a few days after the Christmas tree outing, she found herself remembering the snowball battle—how the children had shrieked with delight when Nathan had come up behind her and sprinkled snow over her head when she wasn't looking. And how his eyes had sparkled as he gently brushed a melting flake away from her cheek.

She leaned on the pitchfork she'd been using to spread fresh hay for Dusty, and gave her thoughts over to the tenderness of that moment. She even allowed her mind to wander into the dangerous territory of remembering how it had felt to be kissed by Nathan.

"Enough," she muttered and went back to work, slinging the hay with such energy that Dusty turned his head and gave her a quizzical look.

"Well, it's ridiculous," she told the ox. "The very idea that he and I..."

Dusty heaved a disgusted grunt and turned back to his water pail.

"Nevertheless, it's true," she argued. "I know so little about the man. Just because he served as a chaplain in the army and just because his sermons stir hearts and minds all around this community, and..."

Dusty shifted impatiently.

"I know exactly what this is," she continued. "It's this early onset of winter and facing weeks and months of isolation and loneliness. This has nothing to do with Nathan Cook, other than that he is a distraction."

Dusty pawed at the fresh hay, ignoring her.

She set the pitchfork aside and trudged back to the house to check on the twins—both of them sick with a stomachache. After a long night of throwing up and moaning in pain, they had both finally fallen into a peaceful sleep. Julianne brushed Luke's hair off his forehead, testing for fever with the back of her hand pressed gently against his cheek. Then she did the same with Laura. Both of them seemed much improved, and she breathed a sigh of relief.

Wanting to let the children sleep, she went back outside. The day was crisp with a bright blue sky and, for once, no wind to chill her to the bone. She walked over to the grove of bur oak trees, gathering sticks and branches that had snapped off. When she heard a harness jingle, she looked up and saw Nathan and Glory coming over the ridge.

Her heart danced with joy at the sight of them—at the sight of *him*. She waved and saw Glory instruct Nathan to leave the trail and head across to the oak trees.

"Sam was at the schoolhouse stoking the fire, and heard the children hadn't come in today," Glory called as soon as she judged herself to be within Julianne's earshot. "Are they sick?"

Julianne nodded. "Stomach," she explained.

Glory nodded. "Thought that might be it. There's something going around. I brought the makings for my chicory tea. It will help ease the tenderness and help them keep down some food."

Nathan halted the team of horses and jumped down. "Here, let me take those," he said relieving Julianne of the bundle of sticks and branches. In spite of the fact that they were both wearing gloves, her breath caught at the sudden nearness of him. He loaded the kindling into the back of the wagon then held out his hand to her, offering her help in climbing onto the seat.

Riding between Glory and Nathan on a seat designed for two people, Julianne had trouble concentrating on the older woman's chatter.

"…thought Nathan might take a ride over your land and help you decide."

"Decide?"

"Where to put the orchard," Glory said, and she pulled off her mitten and placed the back of her hand on Julianne's cheek. "You're not coming down with this thing, are you?"

"No, I'm fine."

They had reached the yard and the cabin door was open a crack. She could see Luke watching them.

"Luke Cooper," Julianne called, "you shut that door and get back in bed now."

"I'll take care of the children," Glory said as Nathan returned from storing the kindling. "You two head on out while you've got a bit of decent weather."

Julianne was well aware that once Glory settled on

a plan, there was no changing her mind, so she scooted herself to the far edge of the wagon seat and waited for Nathan to take the reins.

But the silence that stretched between them as he guided the team and wagon overland was more unsettling than conversation could ever be. Julianne searched for some normal opener and could not believe that the first thing out of her mouth was, "Why did you never marry, Nathan?"

His fingers tightened on the reins and he was looking at the horizon rather than at her.

"I don't mean to pry," she said. "It's just that there was a photo of a young woman among your things."

"Rebecca." He offered no further explanation.

Now that she had brought the subject up, Julianne could not seem to let it go. "Your sister?"

"No." His normally gentle voice was tense, almost angry.

"Then who?"

He heaved a sigh of exasperation. "Rebecca and I were to be married after the war. She promised to wait for me, but I suppose that she had not imagined it would take four years. She did not wait. She married another."

"I'm sorry," Julianne murmured.

"My best friend," he added, as though she had asked.

"I'm sorry," she repeated, and wished with all her heart she had never brought the matter to light. Clearly, he was still in love with the woman. "So your brother is not the only reason you're bound for California?"

"I came west for two reasons. After the years I spent on the battlefield I wanted to find a place where—a place to start fresh."

"And you wish to be reunited with your brother," Julianne added.

His fingers slackened slightly on the reins and the tension in his shoulders eased. "It's important that Jake know he wasn't disowned by everyone in the family— that he still has a brother."

The wave of disappointment that coursed through her veins took Julianne by surprise. Surely it was beneath her to resent a man she'd never known—would never know—a young man who had left home and family because he thought that was his only choice. But if Nathan was to find his brother, he would have to leave Homestead—and her. Come spring, he would move on.

"There," he said pointing to an area where her land bordered the Fosters. "If you put your orchard there between your trees and those Sam planted, and if the Fosters also plant more trees, then you can both have orchards and double the harvest. You could become partners," he suggested.

"That's a wonderful plan, Nathan," she said. She smiled and smoothed the collar of his coat where the wind had ruffled it. He was such a nice man. How any woman could be foolish enough to turn to another when she had the heart of Nathan Cook was beyond Julianne.

"Nathan," she repeated, treasuring the feel of it against her lips. "Sam knows quite a bit about grafting plants and such. He's promised to teach me," she hurried to add, so that the focus shifted from the two of them to the business of raising apples.

"It won't be the same, growing fruit out here, as it was back east," he warned.

"I know, but until the full five years have passed and the land is truly mine, I have to try something." She could not disguise the shiver that rattled through her at the very idea that she could still fail and lose everything.

Nathan thought the shiver indicated that she was cold, and snapped the reins. The team of horses picked their way slowly and carefully across the rutted fields.

"If things don't work out, Julianne," Nathan said, not looking at her, "would you take the children and move back east?"

"To Virginia?"

"That's where your family is, right?"

"The children are my family now," she said, and regretted the hard edge to her voice. "My family has made it clear that they believe I made a mistake in marrying Luke. They would take us in, but it would be with pity and self-righteousness. I will not subject my children to that."

"But where would you go?"

Her laugh rang hollow on the cold air. "Believe me,

Nathan, that is something I think about all the time. As yet, I have no answer."

"Have you prayed on it?"

She swallowed, suddenly aware that this wasn't just any man. This was a man of God. "No," she admitted.

"Why not?"

She shrugged, and to her relief Nathan did not press the matter, but he also said nothing else until they reached her cabin.

"Come in for a moment and warm yourself," she invited as he helped her down.

"No, thank you. I have some business to attend to in town. See if Glory is ready to go. If not, I can come back for her later." He busied himself checking the harness.

"Thank you, Nathan," she said, "for taking the time and for the idea of working with the Fosters and for…"

"My pleasure," he mumbled. "I hope the children are feeling better. And you should get inside and out of that damp cloak before you come down with something yourself."

She knew when she was being dismissed. She just couldn't understand why—and at her own front door.

Chapter Eight

In spite of the good times they had shared over the last several days, Nathan knew that he was being unfair—to himself and to Julianne and the twins. Every activity that brought them closer was only adding to the cost they would all pay when he left in spring. If only she would agree to come with him...

Still, he had promised her children a good old-fashioned Virginia Christmas, and that was exactly what he intended to deliver. After that he would talk to her, and together they would figure out the best way to distance themselves from one another over the winter until he left.

Once he reached town, he stopped first at the mercantile, where he bought the length of ribbon he'd promised Laura and a nickel's worth of candy for Luke. As Jacob Putnam's sister wrapped his purchases, he spotted a piece of soft wood molding behind the counter.

"How much for that piece of molding?" he asked.

Melanie picked up the wood. "It's left over from when

we repaired the counter here. It's just a leftover scrap. Here, take it," she said, and handed it to him. "Another repair at Julianne Cooper's place?"

"Christmas present," he replied, taking his change and pocketing it as he headed for the door. "Mind if I check out back for more scraps of wood?"

"Suit yourself," Melanie replied, then turned her attention to a woman eyeing bolts of fabric behind the counter.

Outside, Nathan found three more cast-off pieces of wood. "These will do nicely," he murmured to himself. So that would take care of Luke. Now for Laura. He frowned. What supplies might a girl need for making a Christmas gift for her mother and brother?

He started past the shop window on his way down the street, and saw Melanie Putnam rolling out yards of fabric for the customer. "Of course, fabric," he said to himself, and reluctantly retraced his steps, knowing that before he could buy the yardage and get back to the Fosters, word would be all over town that Nathan Cook had made some strange purchases that afternoon. But a promise was a promise, and he was not a man to go back on his.

The following afternoon, he arrived at Julianne's homestead about the time he knew that Luke and Laura should be getting home from school. He had tucked the scraps of wood and four assorted squares of fabric into his saddlebag. As he had expected, Luke came barreling out of the cabin the minute he heard Nathan's approach.

"Chore time," he called out and grinned.

"That it is," Nathan agreed, taking note that Julianne did not come to the door as she usually did. "There's some weather approaching," he told the boy. "We'd best get the animals settled in the lean-to as soon as possible. Could be a blizzard, from the looks of that sky."

Luke nodded and went to work. The boy reminded Nathan of his younger brother. Jake was a good ten years younger than Nathan, and before Nathan went off to war, Jake had shadowed his every move, his every action. There was some of that in Luke, Nathan realized as he watched the boy stable the animals.

"Brought you something," Nathan said, and offered the boy the paper sack of candy.

"I thought you forgot," Luke said, his eyes shining as he accepted the bag. "Did you get some ribbon for my sister?"

"I did. I'll make sure she gets it later." Nathan pulled out his pocketknife while Luke returned to his chores. He started slowly whittling a piece of the soft wood.

"Whatcha making?" Luke asked.

"Just whittling," Nathan replied, concentrating on his work. "You ever try it?"

"No, sir. My pa said he'd teach me one day, but…" He shrugged and returned to the task of pitching fresh hay. "I don't even have a knife."

"I could loan you mine," Nathan said. "If you're careful and all."

Luke leaned on his pitchfork and watched Nathan for a long moment. "Would you teach me?"

"I was hoping you might show an interest," Nathan said, handing the boy his knife and the wood he had started to carve into the shape of a spoon. "How about making a spoon for your mother for Christmas?"

"That would be swell," Luke said, as he carved a large chunk of wood from the side of the piece.

"Easy, son," Nathan said, and guided the boy's fingers to move more precisely. "I brought some extra wood along—and some fabric pieces I thought Laura might find a use for. Maybe make your mother a handkerchief."

"We could work on them out here," Luke said. "We could surprise her on Christmas morning."

"I thought that might work. Why don't I go inside and send Laura out to give you a hand? You can let her in on the surprise."

Nathan wanted some time alone with Julianne, and he was sure that the challenge of coming up with handmade gifts for her would keep the twins occupied. "You might want to think about whittling something for your sister, if you have the time."

"And she could make something for me," Luke said.

"Sounds like a good idea."

"Captain?"

Nathan gave the boy his full attention. "Yes?"

"What if I try to whittle something for Ma and I mess it up."

"You won't," Nathan said, "and besides, she'll love it anyway, because you made it."

The boy beamed. "I'm glad you're here," he said, and started to whittle the wood.

"Me, too," Nathan agreed. But as he passed the pile of branches they had collected to build a Christmas tree on Christmas Eve, he firmly reminded himself that he wouldn't always be here. The twins had lost one father, Was he going to rob them of a father figure as well?

Julianne waited until she heard Nathan stamping the snow from his boots before she went to the door. She avoided looking at him.

Nathan removed his hat and coat and hung them on the peg by the door. He smiled at Laura. "Laura, could you give your brother a hand with stabling the animals before the storm hits? I need to talk to your mother for a few minutes."

Laura glanced at Julianne, then pulled on her coat, mittens and shawl and headed out.

"If there's a storm coming, then you shouldn't have ridden all the way out here," she said, and then turned in surprise when instead of taking offense at her scolding, Nathan laughed.

"You're right. I don't exactly have the best sense of direction when it comes to finding my way through a blizzard, do I?"

Julianne could not help but smile. "You've probably learned the route by now," she said.

Nathan sat across from her and cleared his throat.

"I came out today to bring the twins their prizes—the candy and ribbon I promised them."

"You didn't have to do that."

"I also came to see you. I always come to see you," he admitted. "I miss you when I'm not here."

"It's all right. I know you have more things to do than to coddle us—sermons to write and all. Just the other day, when you left you mentioned having to do something," she reminded him.

"I needed to think—work some things out in my mind."

Julianne felt her breath quicken. "And did you?" she asked, picking up her mending.

Nathan chuckled. "I thought I had, but then I was out there with Luke just now and something he said got me thinking another way."

"What was it he said?"

"That he was glad I had come here."

"We all are," Julianne murmured, then looked up and smiled brightly. "I mean, the entire community has benefitted from your being here."

"I'm not thinking about the whole community, Julianne." He stood up and started pacing the small confines of the cabin. "I think you know I have feelings for you, and I think you have some feelings for me as well."

"The children have—"

"I'm not speaking of the children, Julianne. I'm talking about us." He ran his fingers through his thick hair and let out a huff of frustration. "I'm no good at this," he moaned.

Julianne set her mending aside and went to him. She cupped his face in her hands, forcing him to look at her. "You are a good and decent man, Nathan. You have brought laughter back to this house and you have given the children gifts far beyond candy and ribbons. You have helped me find a way to keep this land—this home. I will never forget your kindness and support."

Nathan frowned. "But?"

"But you started on a quest to find your brother. In your heart you made a promise just as I made a promise, to my husband as he lay dying. You set out to find him and reunite with him so that he knew not everyone in his family had abandoned him."

"Come with me," he said, wrapping his arms around her.

"You know that I can't do that. It wouldn't be fair to the children. This is the only home they've ever known. It's the place where their father is buried." She ran her thumbs over his cheeks. "I can't go and you can't stay, so let's give ourselves this time that we have."

She stood on tiptoe and kissed him.

He held her close and whispered. "We can always pray for a miracle," he whispered. "After all, 'tis the season for miracles."

They heard the children outside the front door, stamping their feet and whispering excitedly.

"'Tis also the season for secrets," Nathan said as he loosened his embrace so she could step away before the children burst through the door.

"What have you two been up to?" Julianne asked.

"Chores," Luke mumbled, but then he grinned at his sister and nudged her with his elbow.

Laura giggled.

"I've never known chores to cause you two so much pleasure," Julianne said, winking at Nathan.

"I've got a surprise for you," Luke announced. "I can say my tables all the way to twelve times twelve, which is one hundred and forty-four."

"It's about time," Nathan said, ruffling the boy's hair. "Here it is, just days before Christmas, and Mrs. Foster is still waiting on that turkey."

Julianne sat at the table and Laura and Nathan followed her lead. "Let's hear it," she said.

Luke cleared his throat and began rattling off the numbers. He stumbled only once when he got to six times nine and said fifty-five. Julianne saw Laura signal him to lower the number and he corrected himself and continued. Then he looked at Julianne with a mixture of hope and defeat. "I missed one," he admitted.

"Still, Glory needs that turkey," Nathan reasoned. "Seems to me—"

"You may go," Julianne told Luke, and the boy let out a triumphant shout. "You will mind Captain Cook and Mr. Foster."

"Yes, ma'am," Luke said.

"I wish I could go," Laura said softly.

Julianne wrapped her arm around her daughter's shoulder. "I need you to help me bake a wishing cake," she reminded her.

"What's a 'wishing cake'?" Nathan asked.

Laura grinned. "It's just a cake. But inside we bake a special coin, and whoever gets the piece with coin gets to make a wish."

"What would your wish be?" he asked Laura.

Without a trace of a smile, Laura murmured, "I'd wish that we could stay as happy as we've been today."

"You shouldn't have told," Luke rebuked her. "You're supposed to keep it to yourself."

Laura turned to her mother, her face stricken with worry. "Mama, should I not have told?"

"There's no harm," Julianne assured her. "A wish is the same—spoken aloud or not. It's what you hold in your heart that counts."

"In that case," Luke announced, "my heart just aches for my very own horse. What about you, Captain?"

"Well now, that's a tough one," Nathan said, scratching his head as if deep in thought. "I'd like to find my brother."

"And you will," Julianne said, wondering at her disappointment that his wish had nothing to do with her—with them. And in that moment she realized what she would wish—for him to stay forever. But in spite of the season, Julianne knew from experience that miracles did not happen. Not for her.

Chapter Nine

Two days before Christmas, while the children were in
school, Julianne hitched Dusty to the wagon and headed
to town with a load of her freshly churned apple butter.
She would trade the jars of apple butter to Jacob Putnam
for small gifts for the twins. She felt a hint of excitement
and realized that she was looking forward to Christmas
in a way that she hadn't since she and Luke had left their
families behind.

In the years since they'd settled in Homestead, they
had had to let go of past holiday traditions and establish new ones. They had shared Christmas Eve with the
Fosters, then gone home to trim their tree and lay out
gifts for the children to discover on Christmas morning.
On Christmas Day they had attended church services in
the newly built school. When the circuit preacher could
not be there, men from the congregation would read
scripture passages and the women would lead everyone
in carols. By the time they started for home it would be

dusk, but the twins would still be bursting with excitement, for they knew that after supper their father would cut the wishing cake. He would slice it and pass the slices around the table until a metallic clink told everyone that the coin had been found.

But not last year, she thought, as Dusty ambled along. Last year her husband's grave was still fresh and the children were still trying to understand why God would leave them fatherless. Julianne had not had answers for them, and no one had felt much like celebrating.

"Not this year," she vowed. In spite of her worries that the children were building a bond with Nathan that would devastate them when he left in spring, Julianne was determined to make up for the Christmas the twins had missed the year before. "Plenty of time to wean them from being so close to Nathan over the winter," she assured Dusty as the ox made the final approach to Main Street. "Plenty of time," she repeated, but this time she was thinking of *her* need to distance herself from Nathan over the coming months.

"Any mail?" Nathan asked, as he watched Jacob tally his order. He'd promised himself that he wouldn't ask. Jacob would tell him if something came. Everyone in Homestead knew he was hoping for news of his long-lost brother.

"Over there." Jacob jerked his head toward a small stack of letters and packages strewn haphazardly over a desktop near the front door of the mercantile. On top of the desk was a hand-lettered sign that read: EMMA

PUTNAM, POSTMISTRESS. "We're always a little shorthanded when Emma is down with one of her headaches. Lucinda helps out after school, but some things just don't get done. Have a look."

Nathan swallowed nervously. He'd been disappointed so many times before. The letters he'd sent and the ads he'd run in newspapers out west had produced nothing. And yet he still hoped.

He was vaguely aware that Jacob had continued to talk, but his focus was on the mail. Postponing what he assumed might be the inevitable, he started with the packages, but there were only three of them, and in no time at all he was down to the letters. He picked up the stack and sorted through them quickly. *Get it over with*, he thought, but still his heart hammered with hope.

A shadow passed the window and he glanced up in time to see Julianne walking across Main Street toward the store. He smiled. Whenever God closed one door, he always opened another, and seeing Julianne Cooper was certainly more than enough to compensate for the absence of a letter.

He heard the jangle of the bell over the shop door, and started to replace the stack of letters on the desk when he noticed the envelope on top.

It was addressed to him.

"Captain, are you all right?" Julianne was at his side, her lovely face turned up as she examined him closely. "Why, you've suddenly gone so pale," she said. "Sit down." She indicated the desk chair. "Are you feeling faint?"

He sat, and then grinned at her fanning the envelope between them. "Seems I've got some news," he said softly, indicating, by a glance toward Jacob, who was cutting yardage for two customers, that he wasn't yet ready to have the entire town privy to that news.

Julianne moved so that she was blocking him from the view of the others. "Very well, Captain," she said in a voice just slightly louder than normal conversation. "And the twins as well," she added, pantomiming that he should open the letter while she covered for him. "Of course, they are beside themselves with excitement about Christmas."

Nathan scanned the scrawled note on the single sheet of paper inside the envelope, then handed it to Julianne. He watched her lips move as she read the short note.

Nathan,
Not sure how you found me, but find me you have. I cannot wait for you to come out here. There's work here with the railroad, and once that's built there's land we could buy with our wages. Spring can't come too soon for us, my brother. You head west and watch for the railroad crews building toward the east—I'll be there. Jake

"You found him," she said softly, as she carefully folded the paper and handed it to him. "I'm so happy for you both, Nathan. God has blessed you."

It was true, and yet all Nathan felt was confusion. Wasn't this the news he'd hoped for? Been waiting for all these months? Wasn't this the dream he and Jake had always shared—the dream of working together, building a future together? Weren't those the words he had written in his letters home during the war, never realizing that Jake was long gone and had never seen his letters?

"Nathan?"

He looked up at Julianne and felt his eyes well with tears. He had gotten his wish without the need of a slice of wishing cake, and yet all he could think as he looked up at her sweet face *was I don't want to leave her.*

"Anything?" Jacob called out as he rang up the last sale and glanced toward Nathan. "Ah, morning, Julianne. Did you bring those jars of apple butter?"

"I have them in the wagon," Julianne replied. "I'll get them."

"Let me," Nathan said, pushing himself to his feet and folding the letter into the pocket of his vest.

"Any news?" Jacob asked again.

Nathan hesitated, then patted his pocket. "A letter," he replied, not wanting to lie to the man who'd become his friend. "I'd like some time to study on it," he added.

Jacob nodded. "Understood. And while you're at it—now that you've had news—maybe you'll do some studying on that offer we discussed?"

"I will."

Julianne followed Nathan from the store. "What offer?"

"Jacob and the others are asking me to stay on as

pastor. They're planning to build a proper church, and they want a regular minister."

"Are you considering it?"

Was that hope he saw in her eyes, or was it just more of his wishful thinking? "I was," he admitted, and fingered the edge of the envelope "when there was no word...."

"But now of course, this changes everything," Julianne said as she busied herself uncovering the jars of apple butter she'd packed into wooden crates in the back of the wagon. "It's not really so bad," she reasoned, not looking at him. "I mean, you can't head west until the weather breaks, and in the meantime the church elders can seek a regular minister—run ads, as you did. Someone will come. It's a good opportunity, as is the opportunity your brother has proposed. Work on the railroad must pay well, and think of the farm the two of you could buy together and—"

Nathan stared at her. Who was this woman, babbling like a creek running free after a thaw? "Come with me," he blurted the thought that had been uppermost in his mind ever since reading Jake's letter.

She turned and smiled at him. "Of course I'm coming. I'm bartering with Jacob—the apple butter in exchange for some Christmas presents for the twins and Glory and Sam."

Nathan set down the crate he'd picked up and touched her shoulder. "Not to the store, Julianne. Come with me to California."

"How can I?" she whispered hoarsely, and he realized

that she was every bit as perplexed by the choice as he was. "I also made a promise, Nathan."

"To Luke."

"To my husband and our children," she corrected. "This is our home, Nathan—the only home the twins have really known. After everything they've had to endure this last year, I couldn't…"

He wanted to take her in his arms and assure her that he understood, that he would never ask her to betray a deathbed promise. But they were standing on Main Street, and in spite of the cold weather, people were out—and watching them with curious glances. So he hefted the crate of apple butter to one shoulder and took hold of her elbow with his free hand. "It's Christmas, Julianne. The season of miracles. How about helping me pick out a gift for the Fosters?"

Back inside the store, Nathan set the crate of apple butter on the counter. "There's one more crate," he told Jacob, and headed back outside.

Julianne watched him go, wondering as always at his certainty that things could possibly work out for them. Well, she had been the cause of Luke's break with his family, and she would not come between Nathan and his brother. Jake had been abandoned by his family once, and his letter—however concise the words—had been filled with his delight at having a connection to family once again.

"How can I be of help, Mrs. Cooper?"

Julianne turned to face Jacob. The older man was

always more formal when cast in the role of shopkeeper serving a customer. She pulled a list from her pocket and handed it to him.

"Ah, the ingredients for your wishing cake?"

Julianne nodded. "And I'll need two of those peppermint sticks for the twins," she said, as she focused her attention on the jars of candy that lined the shelf behind the counter. She selected some tobacco for Sam's pipe and a china teapot for Glory, all before Nathan returned with the second crate of apple butter. "Will there be enough to cover all this?" she asked, suddenly aware that she had yet to select an actual gift for the twins—or for Nathan.

"And then some," Jacob assured her as he inventoried the jars and began setting them on a shelf.

Nathan fingered the floral-patterned teapot. "For Glory?"

"Yes. Her favorite teapot was broken when one of the axles on their wagon split on the trip out here. She's never said a word, but every time we come to the store I notice she looks to see if this one is still here."

"What if I gave her the cups and saucers to match?" Nathan asked. "Or maybe not. Maybe that's too—"

"I think she would like that very much."

"I'll need something for Sam."

"He broke the tip on his pocketknife a while back," Jacob said, as he indicated a tray of pocketknives below the glass cover of the counter. "Now, what about those children, Mrs. Cooper? Surely you'll need something beyond the peppermint sticks."

"I was thinking perhaps some paints and brushes for Laura."

Jacob retrieved the items from a shelf near the back of the store. "And young Master Luke?"

Julianne was at a loss. Her son was growing up so fast—both of the children were. She spotted a wooden rocking horse, but Luke was already too big for such a toy, even though his wish had been for a horse of his own.

"How about a hat?" Nathan said, as if reading her mind. "It's not a horse, but it's a start."

"I have just the thing," Jacob said, reaching onto a high shelf for a hatbox printed with a single word: "Stetson". "Young fella by the name of Stetson, from Philadelphia, lived out west of here and came up with an idea for a hat. He went back east and started his own business, but the dandies back there aren't too keen on his design. I picked up half a dozen for next to nothing when Mrs. Putnam and I traveled back east to see family last summer."

He blew the dust off the box cover and pulled it open. "I think this might just be small enough for Luke." He held up a tan felt hat with a high crown and a wide brim. "Waterproof inside and out," he said, "in case Luke finds himself in need of water, with no bucket handy." He made the motion of dipping water from a stream.

"It's dandy," Nathan said, taking the hat from Jacob and perching it on his head.

He looked so ridiculous that Julianne laughed.

"I'm pretty sure I have one in your size as well." Jacob scanned the row of hat boxes.

"Nope. My old one will do me fine," Nathan told him.

"Try it on," Julianne urged. "It will help me imagine what Luke might look like."

Nathan shrugged and accepted the hatbox from Jacob. He pulled out a black version of the wide-brimmed hat and put it on. "I like it," he admitted, adjusting the brim so that the hat fit snugly over his forehead. "Maybe when spring comes." He reluctantly removed the hat and returned it to the box. He turned back to the teacups. "Could you add a couple of those to my tally?"

While Jacob added up the bill, Julianne tried to think of some gift she might choose for Nathan. She looked over the merchant's wares, commenting on this and that and getting absolutely no reaction from the man. She wanted so much to give him something, but she knew that the price of a hat for him, as well as Luke, would be too dear.

"Thanks, Jacob," Nathan said, as he collected his packages, the contents of which were disguised by brown wrapping paper. "Merry Christmas to you and your family."

"And to you," Jacob replied absently, as he gave his attention to wrapping Julianne's purchases.

"Has the captain ever admired anything in particular?" she asked.

Jacob paused in his wrapping and ran one hand over his whiskers. "Not that I can recall. Any time he comes in, it's been to check if there's mail or to get something for the Foster place—or yours. He did seem to like that hat."

"I can't afford two hats, Mr. Putnam."

Jacob considered the hat. "It looked mighty fine on him. Maybe the church elders would agree to give it to him as a token of our appreciation for all he's done since coming here." He winked at Julianne. "You never know. That might just be enough to get him to stay on." He returned to his wrapping. "He'd stay if you asked him," he said after a long moment. "We'd have a full-time preacher and the twins would have a father again."

"Oh, Jacob, that's hardly reason enough to marry. Besides, what would Emma say? She's been trying to match him with Lucinda since he arrived."

"He's not right for my girl."

"Besides," Julianne continued, "he's finally located his brother. It would be selfish of us to want him to stay, when all along his goal has been to be reunited with Jake."

The shopkeeper handed her the parcels and came around the counter to hold the door open for her. "I suppose you're right."

"You know I am. Why, the man has been here only a matter of weeks. We can hardly expect him to change his plans, simply because he's made such an impression on this community. No, we've been given a gift—the gift of having him here for a few months."

"I suppose," Jacob agreed.

But on the drive back to her homestead, Julianne could not help but dwell on Jacob's words. *"He'd stay if you asked him."*

Would he?

"You're being as silly as a lovestruck girl," she admonished herself aloud. "Nathan is attracted to you, but it's different for a man. Men don't fall in love as easily as women do." *As easily as I have*, she thought and she sat upright, tugging on the reins so hard that Dusty stopped in his tracks.

She couldn't be in love with the man, could she? She'd only known him such a short time, and on the heels of Luke's passing at that. No, surely it was his kindness to the children, the way he had helped Glory and Sam, the ministry he had offered the community as a whole. She admired him, and she couldn't deny that he had eased her grief with his sunny disposition and the way he had a habit of turning up whenever she needed help or was feeling down.

Surely, that was all there was to it. It was part of the passage of mourning, part of the path into widowhood, she assured herself. And yet, when she closed her eyes each night, the last thought she had was of Nathan's kiss, his arms—strong and sure—embracing her, and that smile that seemed to say everything would work out.

Chapter Ten

On the morning of Christmas Eve, Nathan and Sam stopped by to pick up Luke so the three of them could go in search of a wild turkey for Glory to cook for their Christmas dinner. Glory came with them, intent on spending the morning with Laura and Julianne preparing pies, corn bread stuffing and spoon bread to serve at their Christmas dinner.

"And don't forget that wishing cake," Nathan called, as he snapped the reins and Sam's team of horses took off.

"Don't let Luke fire your rifle," Julianne shouted back.

And as the horses and wagon disappeared over the rise, she heard Luke's mournful "Oh, Ma," and she laughed.

"Good to hear you laughing again," Glory said, wrapping her arm around Julianne's shoulders. "Love heals all sorrows, that's certain. Big Luke would be happy for you."

Glory and Sam had taken to calling Julianne's late husband "Big Luke" and her son "Little Luke" on the trail out to the territories. The names had stuck.

"Now, Glory, don't you start. Nathan Cook is just a good friend to all of us. That's all."

"Um-huh," Glory sighed. "And next you'll be telling me that tomorrow isn't Christmas Day," she muttered.

The men returned in record time, their laughter and excited voices preceding them on the cold afternoon air.

"We got one," Luke crowed as he held up their bounty for all to see. "I spotted him and Mr. Foster got off the first shot."

"I can see that it's a beauty," Julianne called, trying hard not to meet Nathan's grin or notice his cheeks red with the cold and excitement for her son.

As always, he filled the small room, not because of his size, but because, with him so near, she couldn't seem to concentrate on anything.

"You planning to bake those biscuits or scorch them," Glory asked with a nudge and a nod toward the pan of dough Julianne had absently set on the hot stovetop. "Where's that mind of yours—as if I couldn't guess?" The older woman chuckled with delight and turned to thrust a wooden spoon filled with cornbread stuffing at Nathan. "Taste this."

"Just like home," he said. "Better."

"Julianne's a good cook."

Blushing furiously and hoping everyone would

assume the heat from the fire was the cause, Julianne wiped her hands on her apron and looked around the room. "You know, children, it seems to me this room is missing something."

"The tree," Laura shouted, and Luke echoed her cry. "We have to put it together," they explained in unison to Glory and Sam. "It's going to be the most beautiful tree ever, and we have one for you as well," she confided in a whisper to Glory.

"Put a tree together?" Sam tapped out his old corncob pipe on the hearth. "Where is this tree?"

With the twins leading the way, Nathan and Sam followed them out to the lean-to where they'd stored the two handmade trees. Alone with Glory inside the cabin, Julianne decided to share Nathan's news with her friend.

"Nathan heard from his brother. There was a letter at the mercantile. Jake works for the railroad company, and right now he's living in a camp, waiting for the weather to break so they can continue laying track."

"They're coming west to east then?" Glory continued kneading dough.

"Yes."

"Then knowing his brother is alive and working, Nathan could stay here and wait for Jake to come this way."

"That could be years, Glory. You read the papers. The railroad might not reach us until the next decade. I'd never ask Nathan to wait so long—anything could happen."

"Then go west with him. There's nothing keeping you here—not really."

Julianne wrapped her arms around her friend's thin shoulders. "Only you and Sam and our friends, and this place that I promised—"

Glory wheeled around so that the two women were eye to eye. "Now you listen to me, Julianne, Big Luke would never have wanted you to sacrifice your chance at real happiness for this piece of land. The promise I expect he'd hold you to is the one I heard him ask of you that last night—the one to promise him that you would remarry and make a real home for the twins and yourself."

"He was thinking about here in Homestead, Glory. You know what this place meant to him—and to me," she hastened to add.

"What I know is that living in the past is a pure waste of time and an affront to God Almighty. How many signs do you need, girl?" Glory shook her gently.

Julianne pulled away and turned back to stirring the batter for the wishing cake. "He's asked me about my coming to California with him, but—"

"And you said what?"

"I turned him down. I can't leave and he can't stay, so let's just enjoy this time we have—especially this wonderful Christmas that will be filled with enough memories to sustain us all for years to come."

"Don't know why you'd want to live on memories when you could just as easily have the real thing, but it's Christmas and you're right. Now is not the time to debate the point—we've got all winter for that."

Julianne sighed, knowing her friend would not give up, and nothing she could say would change that. She was relieved to hear the stamping of boots and the giggles of the children outside the front door.

The small, four-foot tree leaned a bit to the left, but it was full and fragrant. Julianne thought she had never seen a more beautiful sight than Nathan standing in the doorway, his arms filled with the branches and snow blowing around his feet, and the twins tugging at his coat as they gave instructions about the trees placement.

"There by the window," Laura said.

"No. Over there," Luke argued, pointing to a spot in the corner. "That way we can see it when we wake up."

"The table," Julianne said quietly. "We're having our main meal tomorrow with Glory and Sam—we can work around it until then."

"Yeah, the table," Luke agreed. "Plenty of room for putting presents under those lower branches if we sit it on the table."

"Table it is," Nathan agreed. "Looks a little bare, don't you think?"

"Wait," Laura said, and ran to get the strings of wild berries she'd been working on and the colorful chain made of scraps of fabric that Glory had insisted she had no use for.

Everyone gathered around the table and dressed the tree. Twice Nathan's fingers touched Julianne's as he handed her part of the berry chain. Twice her fingers lingered on his a beat longer than was absolutely necessary.

"You did a fine job making these trimmings, Laura," Nathan said, and the girl beamed with pride.

"I made something for the tree, too," Luke said shyly. "It's pretty rough but…" He pulled a roughly whittled wooden star out from under his bed covers. "I'll do better next year," he assured them.

Julianne felt tears fill her eyes. "You will do no such thing," she said. "This is our star. It's perfectly wonderful." She hugged both children to her while Nathan worked the star into the top branches, anchoring it with a small box he took from his pocket.

Sam blew his nose and Glory sniffed loudly. "Come on, old man," she ordered. "It's past time we were getting along back. That turkey's not going to cook itself." She kissed the children on their cheeks and squeezed Julianne's hand. "We'll see you tomorrow."

Reluctantly, Nathan followed them to the door, then glanced back at Julianne. "Merry Christmas."

She swallowed around the lump in her throat and rejected the impulse to ask him to stay. "Merry Christmas, Nathan," she managed. "Thanks to you, it's going to be a wonderful Christmas."

After Nathan and the Fosters left, Julianne busied herself getting the children ready for bed. She told them stories until they finally nodded off, then she tiptoed to the wardrobe and pulled down the gifts she'd bought for them and set them under the little tree. While she'd been busy banking the fire for the night, the children had left some gifts on the table as well. One crudely wrapped and misshapen package was addressed "To my sister, from your brother."

Julianne smiled. Next to it were two more gifts, more artistic in their wrapping. Laura had drawn pictures on the plain paper. One gift was for Luke and the other was addressed "To Mama, Love me and Luke." This time she didn't even try to stop the tears, because they were tears of happiness and relief and gratitude for the fact that they had all made it through this long, sorrowful year. Thanks to neighbors who had heard about the plan to turn the farm into an orchard, the deep window ledges were crowded with tin cans filled with dirt and unseen apple seeds that she hoped would blossom into saplings in time for spring planting. Thanks to Glory and Sam, she had managed on her own for a year now. And thanks to Nathan, she had rediscovered her heart.

"Thank you, God," she whispered as she fingered a branch of the tree, setting free its heady perfume. "Thank you for sustaining us through this time of sorrow and for the love of Glory and Sam and for sending Nathan to us."

She paused in her prayer and considered what Captain Nathan Cook had meant to all of them. He had come from five long years of war and despair, and yet his spirit remained positive and strong, so filled with the certainty of better times to come.

"I wish…"

She stopped, horrified at what she'd been about to ask. How many times had she told the twins that prayers were not to be used as substitute for wishes?

She buried her face in her hands. "I love him so," she whispered.

"He would stay if you asked," Jacob had said, and perhaps he would. But was asking him to stay at the expense of reuniting with his brother really love? Wasn't it more a mark of how much she had come to love him that she was willing to let him go? She brushed her tears away with the hem of her apron. "Thy will be done, Lord," she murmured, as she trimmed the wick on the lamp and went to check on the twins.

She had just put on her nightgown and gotten into bed when she noticed the small box nestled at the very top of the tree anchoring Luke's star. It was tied with a green ribbon and there was a small card she had not noticed before. Drawn to the package, she climbed out of bed, wrapping herself in a quilt. She reached up and removed the box, careful not to disturb Luke's star.

"For Julianne...whatever happens, you have won my heart. Nathan"

She untied the thin satin ribbon and opened the box. Inside was a small wooden heart strung on another piece of the green satin ribbon—the perfect length for tying around her neck. She started to put it on but then stopped. She wanted Nathan to tie it around her neck that first time.

"Tomorrow," she whispered, as she placed the small carved heart back in its box. "On Christmas."

Chapter Eleven

Nathan was like a child who couldn't sleep on Christmas Eve. He tossed and turned through the long night. Had she seen his gift? Had she opened it? Would she know it was meant to say so much more than the words he'd finally written on the note?

He slipped out of his bed and dressed in the dark cold of the Fosters' upper loft. As he climbed down the ladder to the main room of the cabin, he could hear Glory and Sam breathing steadily as they slept behind the curtain Glory had devised to give them—and him—privacy. He tiptoed to the door where he pulled on his boots and his coat and hat.

Outside it was still dark, but it had snowed overnight and the white-covered fields gave off a luminescent light. In an hour it would be dawn. By the time he saddled Salt and rode over to her place, Julianne would probably be up and out tending to the morning chores. He checked his pockets for the presents he planned to give the twins, then mounted Salt and rode off across the fields that he had come to know as well as he'd known the way to his father's home back in Virginia.

Home.

It was all that had kept him going those long years of the war. And then he had returned to the place of his youth and found it all gone—the plantation in ruins, his family in disarray and the girl he'd thought would wait for him forever married to his best friend.

But Nathan had gotten through the horror of the war believing one thing—that God had His reasons for everything that happened, and that having faith meant accepting that in time His reasons would become clear. In the meantime, life was short, as he had discovered numerous times on the battlefield, and it was surely a sin not to live out the days given in an attitude of joy and gratitude.

By the time he rode the distance that separated the two homesteads, the sun was starting to rise. It promised to be a splendid day—clear and cold. Nathan saw the curl of smoke before he and Salt topped the ridge and saw the cabin.

As he had imagined, she was out in the yard, scattering feed in a space young Luke had cleared for the chickens. She was wearing the same blue wool dress she'd worn that first Sunday he'd taken the pulpit. She'd covered her head and shoulders with the plaid, woolen shawl that hung with the children's coats next to an empty hook near the door.

That empty hook had held her husband's coat, he was

certain, but recently, and without thinking he had taken to hanging his outer jacket there whenever he entered the house.

He heard the squeals of the children as they threw open the front door waving wrapping paper and the gifts she had left for them. Young Luke proudly modeled the wide-brimmed hat. Nathan couldn't see what Laura was holding, but her smile told him she was just as pleased with the art supplies as her brother was with the hat. He tapped Salt's haunches with his heels and the horse trotted down the ridge toward the cabin.

"Merry Christmas," he called, and the twins turned at the sound and began running to meet him. Julianne did not run with them, but she stopped scattering feed and waited for him to admire the children's gifts.

He dropped the reins and let Luke lead Salt to the hitching post, while he pulled Laura up into the saddle with him. She proudly showed him her collections of brushes and paints. "And there's paper as well," she said. "Mama said we would make it into a sketchbook. All real artists have sketchbooks that they carry with them everywhere," she assured him.

They had reached the cabin and he lifted Laura to the ground then dismounted himself. "Good morning," he said, tipping his hat and scanning Julianne's throat for any sign of the heart he'd carved for her.

"You're out early," she replied, and he wanted to believe that the pink on her cheekbones was shyness because she was sorting through her feelings for him and not the cold. "Come in. We're just about to have some breakfast."

"There are more presents," Luke announced leading the way.

Inside, over bowls of hot barley with milk, the twins exchanged their gifts for each other. With Julianne's, help Laura had knitted Luke a pair of mittens and Luke had carved her name into a rough board. "It's to be the cover of your sketchbook," he explained. "Mama suggested it."

"It's wonderful," Laura gushed, and hugged her brother.

The boy cleared his throat and reached for the last package under the tree. "We got this for you, Mama," he said. "Laura wrapped it, but I helped."

"What could it be," Julianne said, carefully untying the ribbons and folding back the paper that Nathan was certain she would keep as a treasured memory of this Christmas. She held up a wooden spoon and a small bag.

"I carved that for you," Luke told her, "and Laura collected the seeds and made the bag. The captain got me the wood and Laura the fabric."

Julianne peeked inside the bag. "There are so many," she gasped slowly pouring them into an empty bowl. "Wherever did you get so many?"

"When we were peeling the apples and making the apple butter I saved them all," Laura explained, "and so did Glory and our teacher and our friends at school. Everyone helped."

"Now you've got seeds enough to plant apple trees from here to forever," Luke assured her. "And the spoon's for stirring the applesauce and butter that you're gonna make and Laura and I are gonna sell to Mr. Putnam at the mercantile. We're going to be rich," he assured her solemnly, "just like Papa dreamed we would be."

"Oh, children," Julianne managed through her tears as she gathered them to her for a hug, "we're already rich beyond Papa's wildest imagination."

As the children buried their faces against her shoulders, she looked up at Nathan. "There's one more present," she said softly. "I found it last night and now that the captain is here I hope he will do the honors."

Nathan took down the small box from the top of the tree, noticing that the ribbon had been retied. "So you peeked," he teased, laughing with joy when Julianne blushed and nodded.

"What is it, Mama?" Laura asked at the same time that Luke admonished her for peeking. "You told us that wasn't allowed."

Julianne held out her hand to receive the box from Nathan, but instead of giving it to her he opened the lid and took out the necklace.

"Oh, Mama, it's so delicate," Laura cooed, moving in for a closer look.

"You carved this?" Luke asked. "I don't think I could ever do anything so tiny."

"It'll take practice," Nathan said, and reached into his pocket. "This might help." He handed Luke a small pocketknife. "Merry Christmas, Luke. Oh, and Miss

Laura, I didn't forget you." He reached inside another pocket and handed her a small china doll.

"She's so tiny, but look, Mama," Laura exclaimed, "she has real silk hair and eyes that open and close and—"

"What do you say to the captain, children?"

"Thank you," they chorused, hugging Nathan's waist before running to their beds to examine their new gifts.

Nathan held up the necklace. "May I?" he asked.

"I waited for you," she replied, and immediately understood the double meaning of that statement. As he tied the ribbon around her throat and then rested his hands on her shoulders, she covered his hands with hers crossed over her heart. "I will wait for you," she murmured. "If you want. In spring, go west and find Jake, then come back to us. We'll be here waiting."

He thought his heart would beat right out of his chest, it hammered so hard against the bindings of bone and muscle. "Don't promise what you can't know to be true," he murmured against her hair.

She turned and stared up at him. "Nathan, I don't know why that girl you left behind during the war did not wait. What I do know is that her love was not strong enough. Luke and I defied family and friends to come west—we both knew what we were leaving behind, what we were giving up. I know true love when I have it, and I know that I love you with all my heart. God willing, you return that depth of feeling and will come back to us. In the meantime…"

He kissed her then and she kissed him back, until she became aware of the children's muffled giggles and tried to pull away. "The children," she whispered.

"...are going to have to get used to it," he replied and kissed her again before releasing her. "Now then, Master Luke, how about putting on your jacket and that fine new hat and helping me hitch up the wagon. By the time we go by and pick up Mrs. Foster and get to the schoolhouse, it'll be time for services." He didn't have to add that Sam Foster was already at the little schoolhouse getting a fire started and making sure the benches were in place for an overflow crowd.

"What did you give the captain, Mama?" Laura asked when they were all settled in the wagon and on their way to pick up Glory.

"I..." In her excitement over the necklace he'd carved for her, Julianne had completely forgotten to give Nathan the gift she'd made for him. She'd stayed up late for several nights in a row spinning the fine merino wool she'd bartered from Elton Hanson two years earlier, and then never used because Luke had fallen ill. After his death there had seemed no purpose for such fine wool.

But even in spring, Nathan would need the warmth of a scarf, and she hoped that such a fine one would remind him of her—would eventually bring him back to her.

"You said you were making him something from all of us," Laura reminded her. "You didn't forget, did you?"

"No. I... Oh, Nathan, I do apologize. Your gift is back at the cabin."

"No matter," he replied cheerfully. "Gives me a good reason to come calling later this evening. Besides—" he winked at Laura "—I'm still hoping to get that wishing coin in my piece of cake today. That would sure enough be a fine present, especially if I get my wish."

"Don't tell," Luke warned.

"He knows that," Laura said. "There's Mrs. Foster," she cried, waving wildly. "I can't wait to show her my doll."

Suddenly it occurred to Julianne how Glory would view the necklace that Nathan had given her. She fingered the small carved heart and considered tucking it beneath the high collar of her dress.

But then she saw Nathan watching her and knew that he had read her thoughts. He had given her far more than a token that morning. The man had offered her his heart, and regardless of what anyone thought, she wasn't about to hide it. She straightened the necklace so that the heart was perfectly centered—and perfectly obvious to everyone. And she couldn't help noticing that a breath of relief preceded the smile Nathan gave her as she scooted closer to him to make room for Glory.

Nathan had worked for nearly two weeks on his sermon for the Christmas service. He wanted to give the people of Homestead a sense of what they meant to him, of how they had taken in this stranger and made a place for him in their community and their hearts. How they had trusted him to lead them in worship and how

FREE Merchandise is 'in the Cards' for you!

Dear Reader,

We're giving away FREE MERCHANDISE!

Seriously, we'd like to reward you for reading this novel by giving you **FREE MERCHANDISE** worth over **$20.** And no purchase is necessary!

You see the Jack of Hearts sticker above? Paste that sticker in the box on the Free Merchandise Voucher inside. Return the Voucher promptly … and we'll send you valuable Free Merchandise!

Thanks again for reading one of our novels – and enjoy your Free Merchandise with our compliments!

Jean Gordon

Jean Gordon

P.S. Look inside to see what Free Merchandise is **"in the cards"** for you!

We'd like to send you two free books to introduce you to the Love Inspired® Historical series. These books are worth over $10, but they are yours to keep absolutely FREE! We'll even send you 2 wonderful surprise gifts. You can't lose!

REMEMBER: Your Free Merchandise, consisting of **2 Free Books** and **2 Free Gifts**, is worth over $20.00! No purchase is necessary, so please send for your Free Merchandise today.

Plus TWO FREE GIFTS!

We'll also send you two wonderful FREE GIFTS (worth about $10), in addition to your 2 Free Love Inspired Historical books!

Order online at:
www.ReaderService.com

YOUR FREE MERCHANDISE INCLUDES...

2 FREE Love Inspired® Historical Books

AND 2 FREE Mystery Gifts

▼ DETACH AND MAIL CARD TODAY! ▼

(LIH-FM-10R)

and ® are trademarks owned and used by the trademark owner and/or its licensee. © 2009 Steeple Hill Books. Printed in the U.S.A.

FREE MERCHANDISE VOUCHER

**2 FREE
BOOKS**
and
**2 FREE
GIFTS**

Please send my Free Merchandise, consisting of
2 Free Books and **2 Free Mystery Gifts.**
I understand that I am under no obligation to buy
anything, as explained on the back of this card.

*About how many NEW paperback fiction books
have you purchased in the past 3 months?*

❑ 0-2
E4GT

❑ 3-6
E4G5

❑ 7 or more
E4HH

102/302 IDL

FIRST NAME	LAST NAME

ADDRESS

APT.#	CITY

STATE / PROV.   ZIP/POSTAL CODE

Offer limited to one per household and not valid to current subscribers of Love Inspired® Historical books. **Your Privacy**—
Steeple Hill Books is committed to protecting your privacy. Our Privacy Policy is available online at www.ReaderService.com
or upon request from the Reader Service. From time to time we make our lists of customers available to reputable third parties
who may have a product or service of interest to you. If you would prefer for us not to share your name and address, please
check here ❑. **Help us get it right**—We strive for accurate, respectful and relevant communications. To clarify or modify your
communication preferences, visit us at www.ReaderService.com/consumerschoice.

NO PURCHASE NECESSARY!

The Reader Service - Here's how it works:
Accepting your 2 free books and 2 free mystery gifts places you under no obligation to buy anything. You may keep the books and gifts and return ~
shipping statement marked "cancel." If you do not cancel, about a month later we'll send you 4 additional books and bill you just $4.24 each in the ~
or $4.74 each in Canada. That's a savings of 20% off the cover price. It's quite a bargain! Shipping and handling is just 50¢ per book.* You may can ~
at any time, but if you choose to continue, every other month we'll send you 4 more books, which you may either purchase at the discount price ~
return to us and cancel your subscription.

   *Terms and prices subject to change without notice. Prices do not include applicable taxes. Sales tax applicable in N.Y. Canadian residents will ~
charged applicable provincial taxes and GST. Offer not valid in Quebec. All orders subject to approval. Books received may not be as shown. Credi ~
debit balances in a customer's account(s) may be offset by any other outstanding balance owed by or to the customer. Please allow 4 to 6 weeks for ~
livery. Offer available while quantities last.

BUSINESS REPLY MAIL
FIRST-CLASS MAIL   PERMIT NO. 717   BUFFALO, NY

POSTAGE WILL BE PAID BY ADDRESSEE

THE READER SERVICE
PO BOX 1867
BUFFALO NY 14240-9952

NO POSTAGE
NECESSARY
IF MAILED
IN THE
UNITED STATES

If offer card is missing, write to The Reader Service, P.O. Box 1867, Buffalo, NY 14240-1867
or visit: www.ReaderService.com

they had rewarded him by asking him to stay—even though they knew he could not.

If only there were some way…

But he had made a promise and Jake had had enough heartache in his young life without Nathan breaking his word to him. The letter Jake had sent had been filled with dreams for the two of them to start over in a new place together. And wasn't that exactly what Nathan had hinted at in the letters he'd sent home before Jake left?

He hadn't counted on meeting Julianne. He hadn't counted on loving her and her children. He hadn't counted on finding a home in a place he'd barely heard of. After the war and the discovery of his sweetheart's betrayal, Nathan had focused on making life better for Jake, but God had had other plans, and now Nathan had no idea which path to follow, for either way he went seemed destined to lead to heartbreak for someone he loved.

Chapter Twelve

Nathan's sermon was so moving that it brought tears to Julianne's eyes. For the first time since Luke's death, she allowed herself to face squarely the truth of his final days. Luke's toes and fingers had been badly frostbitten by the time they found him that terrible night, and he had cried out in anguish with the pain that followed. Glory and Sam had taken the twins to their place so they wouldn't hear their father's suffering, but even after the initial agony had passed, there had been little hope that Luke would ever again be able to farm the land or walk without considerable help. The idea that he would teach young Luke to hunt and fish was out of the question.

And on Christmas Day, sitting next to Glory on the rough-hewn bench that she and Luke had shared with the Fosters, Julianne finally opened her heart to the truth. In taking Luke, God had shown not vengeance but mercy. For Luke had always been such an active man, so filled with energy, that to live for years dependent on the help of others would have surely been a slow and torturous death.

She saw that in sending Nathan to her door under similar circumstances to how Luke had left her, she had been given a new opportunity—to live, to love and to fulfill the very legacy Luke had been so intent on leaving for his children. Nathan had given her all of that, and she realized now that God's hand had been at the helm of all that had happened since Nathan had arrived.

To wish that he could stay—that they could be together—was simply selfish, and yet...

There had to be a way. *Please, God,* she prayed when Nathan called for a moment of silent prayer, *show us that path.*

She fingered the small carved heart as she prayed, her eyes tightly shut, her lips moving. Only when Glory placed her hand on Julianne's knee did she realize that her tears were flowing freely and that she felt such a release of all the pain and bitterness she had held inside for over a year.

"Amen," Nathan intoned, ending the silent prayer. "And now, as we leave this place for the hearths of home and family that sustain us all, join me in singing 'Silent Night', and may the carol's words echo across these high plains throughout this blessed day."

Slowly, people filed out of the schoolhouse-turned-chapel. They exchanged greetings and farewells with a nod of their heads or the raising of their hands. No words were spoken because everyone was either singing or humming the carol, and as Nathan had suggested, the sounds of their voices mingled with the sound of bells laced onto the harnesses of horses and oxen and drifted over the rises of the fields as they all went their separate ways.

Just outside the schoolhouse, Nathan fell into step with Julianne and the twins, his strong baritone blending with their higher voices as he helped them into the wagon.

On Christmas Day, the Fosters had established a tradition of opening their home to anyone who did not have extended family with whom to share the day. So it was hardly surprising to see several wagons pulled into the yard by the time Nathan and Julianne arrived. The twins ran off to join the children of a young couple who had recently settled in the area, while Nathan helped Julianne carry in the baskets of cookies and puddings she had made to contribute to the feast.

Inside the cabin, everyone seemed to be talking at once as Sam served up mugs of newly pressed apple cider and Glory made room on the table for what seemed an unending stream of side dishes brought by her guests.

"We'll be eating until the New Year arrives," she exclaimed happily as each new dish was unveiled.

The children settled on the floor near the hearth to play a game of pickup sticks with a pile of wood splinters that Sam had gathered for them. Julianne busied herself helping Glory and tried without much success to avoid stealing looks at Nathan.

"You two need to figure this thing out, and sooner

rather than later," Glory muttered when the two women went outside to collect more kindling for the fire. "He must have worked on that necklace most of the night, once he got started on it. Had to begin again at least three times I know of, because the work was so fine he kept breaking it. Wouldn't have done to give you a broken heart, now would it? Although it seems to me you both might be headed toward having your hearts broken if you don't find some way to get together."

"He's given me this token of his devotion, Glory, and God willing, someday we will find a way to be together."

"These are hard times, child, and the one thing life should have taught you so far is that you cannot count on having forever. You and Nathan need to work this business out now." She glanced toward the cabin as Nathan stepped outside. "And I'll leave you to it."

Glory muttered something to Nathan on her way back inside that made him smile. "I think Glory is growing impatient with us," he said, as he removed his coat and wrapped it around Julianne's shoulders.

"She doesn't understand, but I do, Nathan. You made a promise to Jake and you need to honor that promise. Once you've done that—"

"I've been thinking," Nathan interrupted her, running his finger along her cheek. "I made a promise to find Jake and let him know he still had family. Jake and I know where the other one is and there's no possibility we can be together for months to come. I'll be staying here until at least April, and frankly, Julianne, I may be a man of the cloth, but I'm not sure I can be here for that length of time and not be with you."

"You see me and the children practically every day," she protested, but she would not look at him.

He gently lifted her face to his. "You know what I'm saying, what I'm asking, Julianne. Will you marry me?"

"I also have a promise to keep," she reminded him.

"To your late husband."

"To my children. The land Luke and I have home-steaded is their future, their legacy, their connection to their father. I cannot just abandon that and start over in California."

"I understand. So I was thinking that perhaps we could marry, and then, once the weather turns, we could go together to California—a wedding trip."

"But Jake's letter spoke of you working together, earning the money you need to start your own business in California."

Nathan shrugged. "That's his dream. Mine is right here. I love you and I've come to care deeply for the twins. Will you marry me, Julianne?"

Her heart screamed *Yes!*, but she had to consider the children. Although it was obvious that they liked Nathan and looked forward to his visits, that was a very different matter than having him become part of their family. "I…"

"The children, right?"

She nodded. "They're so young, and they've had so much to deal with this last year."

"If they were in favor, would you say yes?"

It was as if the nodding of her head was completely out of her control.

Nathan grinned. "Then I'll ask the children to marry me as well." Just as he leaned in to kiss her, the laughter and sounds of celebration from the house spilled out into the yard, as the children broke free of the stuffy interior to play outside.

Luke threw the first snowball, missing his target and hitting Nathan squarely in the back instead.

Nathan smiled, kissed Julianne on the nose and bent to scoop up a handful of snow. "Better head for cover," he told Julianne. "There are seven of them, and this could take a while."

Julianne held his coat out to him. "If you insist on playing little-boy games, at least put this on," she ordered.

"See? You're talking like a wife already."

Julianne reached up and shook the canvas that Sam had hung to protect his woodpile from the elements, sending a shower of snow down on top of Nathan.

"Hey," he shouted in protest as she ran for the house.

The dinner was a feast worthy of kings by any measure. By the time Laura carried the wishing cake to the table and set it in front of Julianne for slicing, there was a chorus of protests.

"I really couldn't eat another bite."

"Perhaps later."

But seeing the disappointment that shadowed the faces of the children, the adults gave in. "Maybe just the smallest slice."

As Julianne sliced the cake, the pieces were passed to her right and around the table, all the way to the guest on her left. More than half the table had been served before she heard the telltale clink of the coin on the plate.

The room went still.

"It appears that the captain will get his Christmas wish," Sam said with a sly grin, as he handed Nathan the plate. "Care to share the wish?"

"Nope. I understand it won't come true if I tell." He winked at Luke and Laura. "Maybe tomorrow," he added, as his gaze met Julianne's. "I mean, if it comes true, then what's the harm in telling?" He glanced at the twins and then back to her.

"No harm at all," Sam replied, nudging Glory as he took a bite of cake.

Nathan saw Julianne and the children home. He wanted to talk to the twins, but had found no opportunity to do so at the Fosters'. Once they reached Julianne's cabin, she told the children to get into their nightclothes and she would make them all some hot milk with vanilla.

She was nervous. "Maybe it would be better to talk to them later," Julianne whispered, as she stirred vanilla into the milk. "They've had such an exciting day already, and well, what if…"

"We won't know if we don't talk to them," Nathan

replied. "Would you rather talk to them yourself? I can leave." Of course, he knew he wouldn't get a wink of sleep if she said that would be the best plan.

"No. We should talk to them together."

"Why are you whispering?" Luke asked, then he grinned. "I know. There's another Christmas secret, isn't there?"

"Not a secret exactly," Nathan said, glancing over the boy's head to seek Julianne's help.

"Children, Captain Cook and I have something we want to discuss with you." Julianne set their cups of warm milk on the table.

"It's a bad thing, isn't it?" Laura said, her eyes tearing up. "Like when Papa was—"

"No," Nathan assured her. "It's nothing like that." He pulled her stool closer to his. "Come and drink your milk and we'll tell you."

The children looked warily from one adult to the other, but did as they were told.

Julianne handed Nathan his cup of milk, then turned back to the stove to fill her cup.

"I've been spending a lot of my time here these last weeks and I've come to care about you and your mother a great deal," Nathan said.

"As we have come to care for the captain," Julianne added, taking her seat at the table.

"You're our friend," Luke said with a shrug, "you know, like Mr. and Mrs. Foster are our friends and..."

Laura patted Nathan's hand. "We like you," she assured him.

This was not going to be as easy as Nathan had hoped. "Well, sometimes when grown-ups get to be friends, they realize that they would like to be even closer—more than just friends or neighbors."

"Oh, you mean like when you kissed Mama? Like mushy stuff?" Luke said, his eyes wide with understanding but at the same time some puzzlement.

Laura clapped her hands together excitedly. "You're getting married? Is that the secret? Was that your wish today when you got the wishing coin?" She looked at her mother expectantly.

"Would you children be all right with that?" Julianne asked.

"Of course," Laura said. "Just think—Christmas and now a wedding? It's wonderful!"

Luke remained quiet and seemed to have taken a great interest suddenly in studying the sparks of the fire.

"Luke?" Nathan said quietly. "What do you think?"

"You'd be our Papa?"

"Only if you chose to call me that someday," Nathan said. "I would be married to your mother and we would all live here together. We would take care of the farm your papa started, and one day the land would officially be your mother's, and after that it would come to you. Just as your father intended."

"I thought you had to go find your brother and live in California," Luke continued, still not looking directly at Nathan.

"I had an early Christmas surprise a week or so ago.

I had a letter from my brother. He's working on building the railroad that might one day run right through Homestead."

"If the captain and I were to marry—if we were to become a family—then perhaps in the spring we could all go out to California and meet Mr. Jake."

"He'd be our uncle, right?" Laura said, her eyes ablaze with excitement.

"In a manner of speaking," Nathan said. "Luke?"

The boy looked at his mother. "We'd be a family again?"

She nodded.

"And I could learn to do all the stuff that Papa promised he'd teach me one day?"

Another nod. "And with the captain living here, I expect I wouldn't need quite so much help from the two of you," Julianne added. "Although you would still have chores," she hastened to add.

Nathan reached out and touched each child. "So, what I'm asking the two of you to think about—and you don't have to answer right away—is if it would be all right if your mother and I married and I came here to live."

"Are you still going to preach at the church?" Luke asked.

"If they still want me."

"Luke," Laura said, sidling closer to her brother, "let's say yes. Mama loves the captain and he likes us a whole lot, I think."

"Miz Putnam is always talking about how I'm the man of the family since Papa died," Luke said, looking directly at Nathan for the first time. "Would you be willing to take that on? Because I've got to tell you, there's a lot of worrying and stuff to go with that."

"I'll keep that in mind," Nathan said, trying hard not to smile.

The children sipped their milk and eyed each other over the rims of their cups. Julianne appeared to be holding her breath. Nathan sent up a silent prayer that they were doing the right thing in asking the twins, even if they said no.

Laura made a gesture with her fingers. Luke responded with a nod. "It'll be all right," he said. "I reckon we'll make a good family."

Julianne's breath came out on the wings of her smile. Laura was also beaming. But Nathan solemnly offered Luke his hand. "You won't regret this," he said as he shook Luke's hand and then Laura's.

"We're going to be married," Laura said happily. "I can't wait."

"Neither can I," Nathan admitted, his eyes resting on Julianne's beautiful face. "How about New Year's Day?"

"So soon?"

"No reason to wait that I can think of," Nathan said. "Luke? Any reason to wait?"

"No, sir."

"But," Julianne started to protest. "There's so much to do, and—"

"Miz Foster and the other ladies will help, Mama,"

Laura told her. "Let's get married right away so we can be a real family again."

"Will you attend me, Laura?" Julianne asked, and the girl started to tear up again, but this time they were tears of joy.

"Come to think of it, I'm going to need somebody standing up for me," Nathan added, as he placed his hand on Luke's shoulder.

"Do I have to wear an itchy suit?"

"I sure hope not," Nathan assured him. "I don't have a suit, so my Sunday shirt and maybe a new pair of trousers is going to have to do."

"I'll wear my hat," Luke decided. "You should get one, too."

"I'll look into it," Nathan said as he raised his cup. "Shall we toast our decision?"

The four cups met over the center of the rough-hewn table, where Nathan hoped they would share meals and conversations and happy decisions like this one for years to come.

Chapter Thirteen

Julianne soon discovered that planning a wedding on the prairie in the middle of winter was a convoluted affair to say the least. In the first place, the citizens of Homestead had come from all manner of communities and cultures back east, and every woman had her own ideas about how the wedding should be handled.

"You'll naturally need to reserve the school for that day, and there's the matter of floral decorations," Emma said, as she ticked off items on her fingers. "My sister Melanie is quite adept at arranging flowers. Will you need a bouquet for Laura as well as yourself, dear?"

Julianne opened her mouth to answer, but Emma wasn't listening.

"Are you quite sure you wouldn't prefer to have someone—well, more mature—attend you? It's a responsibility as well as an honor after all. And what will you wear?"

"In our homeland of Germany," Margot Hammerschmidt interrupted, "it is quite common for the guests to kidnap the bride before the wedding so that the groom must search for her."

"That's barbaric," Lucinda Putnam exclaimed.

Glory rolled her eyes. "And how, may I ask, is that any more uncivilized than grown men racing each other to the bride's house for the reception, just so they can be the first one there and win a kiss from the new bride?"

Emma tapped her pen impatiently on the counter. "We were discussing what our dear Julianne is to wear." She studied the shelves behind her that held bolts of fabric in all the colors of the rainbow.

"I can wear my Sunday green," Julianne said. "At least that's one decision we don't have to fret about."

"Absolutely not," Emma exclaimed. "I will not hear of it." She took down a bolt of fine wool in a pale rose. "White is out of the question, of course, but this…"

Glory ran her palm over the fabric. "It's beautiful." She unwound several yards and let the fabric spill over her tall frame. "Look how it drapes."

Julianne lightly ran her fingers over the fabric. She couldn't help thinking how Nathan's eyes would light up, seeing her in such a beautiful gown. But he would love her no matter what she wore, and the price of fabric, not to mention the time it would take to sew the gown, was just impractical.

"No," she said firmly, and turned her attention to the bolts of lace trimmings. "Perhaps a lace cap."

"That, too," Glory said, testing the rose wool against

several of the lace patterns. "Something a little heavier, I should think." She looked at the other women who all nodded in agreement.

"Yes, that cream is perfect," Margot said. "Come over here, Julianne, and let me see it against your skin in the daylight."

Before Julianne could stop them, her friends had gathered around, draping the rose fabric over her shoulders and letting it flow to the planked floor of the mercantile, and then unfurling several feet of the lace to cover her golden hair.

"Perfection," Lucinda murmured. "The captain will be quite overcome when he sees you."

All of the women giggled like young girls, and Julianne could not help smiling. "I suppose I could sell—"

"You will sell nothing," Emma exclaimed, her expression one of horror. "This is our wedding gift to you, dear. Am I not right in saying that, ladies?"

The others nodded. "I think six yards will do," Glory announced, laying the bolt of wool on the counter and measuring out the yardage.

"And perhaps two of the lace?" Margot suggested.

Again, nods all around, and Julianne accepted their incredible generosity, for she understood that it allowed them to play an active role in the wedding—and what woman didn't enjoy that?

"Thank you all so much," she said, hugging each of her friends in turn. "You have made me so happy."

"Well, that was the point," Emma huffed. "Now, we

have a good deal of work to complete, ladies. Shall we divide the tasks?"

In short order, Emma had handed out the assignments. Glory would make the gown with Lucinda's help. Melanie was to take charge of flowers and Margot the making of the headpiece.

"And you, Mother?" Lucinda asked.

Emma sighed. "I shall do what I always do, child. I shall make sure it all gets done."

All of the women burst into laughter, and after a moment of trying to hold her composure, Emma joined them. These dear women had become more than just her friends, Julianne realized—they were more like family.

The days seemed endless to Nathan, in spite of the fact that Julianne hinted that there simply were not enough hours to do everything that needed to be done for the wedding. What did he care of flowers and food and music and such? All he wanted was to stand before the makeshift altar and pledge himself to Julianne—and the twins—for the rest of his days.

"Who will say the words?" Franz Hammerschmidt asked one morning, as the men gathered around the stove in the mercantile, their feet stretched out toward the stove. This was a winter morning ritual, as they smoked their pipes and cigars and considered the problems of the day. "You can hardly marry Julianne and stand in the pulpit at the same time," the German farmer reasoned.

"I could do it," the circuit judge, Matthew Farns-worth, said. "If you can't get the circuit preacher here in time, I have to power to perform weddings."

"We figured, if he couldn't make it on New Year's we'd just delay the wedding a week or so, but Mrs. Cooper and I would be honored to have you marry us, sir," Nathan said. "After all, she was so grateful for your counsel regarding the orchard and how it would qualify as a crop."

Jacob poured himself a tin cup of coffee from the pot on top of the stove. "We're all going to have to stop calling your bride by her former name," he reminded Nathan, and all the men chuckled.

Julianne Cook, Nathan thought and smiled.

"What about the twins?" Another man asked. "You planning to adopt them and give them your name as well?"

"That'll be up to them," Nathan said, and he did not miss the way the other men glanced at each other in surprise. In their world, the man was the head of the household, the one who made the decisions that mat-tered. But Nathan had considered the way Julianne had been pretty much on her own for the last year. Would it be fair to suddenly walk into her cabin—her life—and expect to simply take over?

"The twins will have time enough to get used to having me around full-time," he told the others. "No need to rush anything."

Several of the others nodded as if Nathan had pre-sented a concept they had never contemplated, but one that seemed to have some merit.

"Any of those seeds the ladies planted for Julianne showing signs of life?" Jacob asked, after the group had sat in comfortable silence for a long moment.

"Not so far," Nathan admitted.

Franz frowned. "It's been what—three weeks?"

"Something like that. They'll come along," he said. "It's a long winter." But he couldn't help wondering what he would do if the seeds did not germinate. The fields would have to be planted, and he knew very little about such things. Before the war he had studied to become a minister.

"You could move into town once we get the church built," Jacob said, as if reading his mind. "I don't see why we shouldn't build a little house behind the church—a parsonage."

"No. We'll live on that land," Nathan told them firmly. "And we'll make it work."

Sam Foster nodded approvingly. "And you can count on us to be there to give you a hand," he said.

Jacob cleared his throat and took down a large hatbox from a shelf near the circle of friends. "Nathan, we thought maybe you could use this—consider it a wedding present, if you like. The main reason is that we wanted to find some way to let you know that we're real pleased you're going to stay and fill the pulpit for us permanently."

Nathan opened the box and took out the black Stetson. "It's a perfect fit," he said, as he tried it on, "just like me, with all of the good people of Homestead. I thank you, gentlemen, for everything."

* * *

Later that evening, while Julianne told the children a story and tucked them in, Nathan couldn't help surveying the cluster of tin cans that cluttered the two deep window wells. Each can was filled with dirt. Each can was carefully labeled with the date of planting. Not one showed the slightest sign of life.

He was so deep in thought about the responsibility he would be taking on in just two days that he was startled when Julianne came up behind him, wrapped her arms around his waist and laid her cheek against his back.

"You're very quiet tonight," she said, her voice muffled against his shirt.

He turned so that he could hold her. "Just thinking about the day after tomorrow," he said, forcing a lightness into his voice that his anxiety for their future could not entirely disguise.

Julianne look up at him. "Nathan, we don't have to do this, you know. If you're having second thoughts about the promise you made to Jake—about…"

He kissed her. "Shhh," he whispered against her hair. "I fulfilled that promise. I found Jake and we are in touch. In the spring you and I will go west and make sure that he is well settled and at peace."

"And if not?"

"Then we will bring him back here with us. He is my brother, Julianne, but you are going to be my wife, and the twins will be our children. I will not abandon my family as my father did his."

"He didn't really—"

"Yes, he did. He left Jake no choice but to leave. He was always so insistent on being right."

"Still, from everything you've told me, he was a good provider—a God-fearing man."

"And that is where he and I differed. The god he followed was an angry and vengeful god."

"And what do you believe, Nathan?"

"I believe that, when all else seems lost, our faith can see us through anything—war, the loss of loved ones. Anything. God is love, Julianne. I believe that with all my heart."

He did not ask the question uppermost in his mind. *What do* you *believe?* He knew that she and her first husband had been devout churchgoers and that after Luke's death she had made sure the twins attended church regularly. But what did she believe?

As if she had read his mind, she cupped his face in her palms. "There was a long period after Luke died when I turned my back on my faith, Nathan. I locked my heart away and refused to allow myself to be comforted by the words of the scriptures or the teachings of the minister who conducted services."

"And now?"

"That first Sunday, when you spoke about the losses of war, I felt something. It was as if there had been the slightest loosening of bonds that had held me so tight for all the months since Luke's death."

"What was it you felt that day?"

"When you spoke about the war and the things you had seen, I felt as if finally someone understood. I felt for the first time in months that I was not alone."

"But you were never alone. You had Glory and Sam and—"

"Spiritually speaking, I was alone because I had made that choice. Remember that day you came here to ask what I had thought of your service? I did not tell you that I had for the first time in all those long and terrible months thought about others who had suffered, instead of dwelling only on my own suffering and that of my children."

Nathan hugged her to him. "You are going to be a wonderful preacher's wife," he said.

She laughed and tweaked his nose. "Let's see how I do as *your* wife before I have to live up to such a lofty title as 'preacher's wife'."

"I love you, Julianne. I promise you—"

She placed her forefinger against his lips. "Sh-hh," she whispered. "No need for promises. Love is enough."

And, in that moment, Nathan had never been more sure that God had led him to this place, this woman, and the sacred promise of the life they would share.

For January, the weather was unusually mild—above zero, according to Sam, who had arrived early to take Julianne and the twins to town. There, Julianne was to change into her wedding finery at the Putnam home, and then Jacob and Emma would drive her and the twins to the school, once Sam had assured them that Nathan was waiting inside with Judge Farnsworth.

"It does not do for the groom to see the bride on their wedding day," Emma had lectured both Julianne and

Nathan at the dinner Glory gave for them the evening before.

"Why not?" Luke asked. "They see each other all the time."

"It's simply tradition," Emma told him.

"And traditions don't always make a lot of sense," Sam added, "but you learn not to question them."

Luke shook his head and rolled his eyes. "Grown-ups," he muttered.

"Of which you will be one someday, young man," Emma said, effectively silencing the boy, who had clearly never considered this.

Now, as Julianne put on the beautiful, rose-colored gown Glory had stitched for her, and turned so that Emma could place the lace headpiece over her curls, she found herself thinking years into the future. She saw Nathan walking Laura down the aisle of the new church the town planned to build. She imagined other children—those she and Nathan would have together, attending their older sister. She saw Luke, serious and proud like his father had been, with a home and family of his own.

"I'll get your flowers," Emma said with a sigh that said, if she didn't do everything herself it would not get done. Alone with Glory, Julianne stared at her reflection in the mirror.

"I never imagined," she whispered.

"That you would marry again?"

"That I could be so happy," Julianne corrected, her eyes welling with tears of joy as she hugged her friend.

"Now stop that," Glory fussed, wiping away tears from Julianne's cheeks with her thumbs. "You have surely been blessed to come to this day, and it's a blessing we all share in seeing you and those dear ones embarking on this new life together."

"The sleigh is here," Luke bellowed from the foot of the stairs.

"Off you go," Glory said, giving Julianne one last quick hug.

The school had been transformed with ribbons and candles. Laura was holding a nosegay made of dried herbs, and in the vestibule of the school Emma handed Julianne a similar bouquet, enhanced by sprigs of evergreen.

"Ready?"

Julianne nodded and Emma opened the doors a crack and signaled the organist. As soon as they heard the whoosh of the pump organ's bellows, Emma opened the door fully and signaled Laura to start down the short aisle.

Luke moved to Julianne's side and offered her his arm as Emma had taught him to do. "Ready?" he asked and grinned up at her.

Julianne was through the door and partway down the aisle before she looked up and her eyes met Nathan's. In his gaze she saw so much—the days and months and, God willing, years they would share. The children she hoped they would raise together. The community they would embrace and help build. And most of all the blessing God had bestowed upon both of them.

God had not turned His back on her, she realized, as she had thought when Luke died. She was the one who had turned away. God had been there all along, patiently waiting for her to come back to the faith of her childhood.

When she was almost to him, Nathan stepped forward and took her hands in his, and together with Laura and Luke, the four of them walked the rest of the way together.

The moment the judge pronounced them husband and wife the hall erupted with noisy celebration. The organist pulled out the organ stops assuring the sound would crescendo to its full volume. On both sides of the aisle, women laughed and chattered and men grinned and clapped each other on the backs as if they had just seen a favorite son married. And in the midst of it all, Nathan beamed down at Julianne as if he simply could not believe his good fortune.

"You're supposed to go," Luke coached, tugging on Nathan's trouser leg. "Miz Putnam said—"

"First they have to kiss," Laura corrected her brother, "and then they leave."

The twins looked up at their mother expectantly.

"Miz Putnam has spoken," Nathan said, and held out his arms to her.

When they kissed there was a shout of approval from the men and shushing from the women, but when they turned to make their way back up the aisle, everyone was smiling at them and several women were dabbing at their eyes with lace handkerchiefs.

Emma had insisted that she and Jacob host the wedding reception. "Your home is serviceable, Julianne, but hardly large enough for such occasions. Besides, this way those fools intent on racing to be the first to kiss the bride will have a shorter distance in which to break their necks."

As it turned out, Sam Foster was the first man through the door, other than the bridal couple and their hosts. He seemed inclined to ignore the tradition, but young Luke called him on it.

"You have to kiss Mama—it's tradition," the boy instructed.

Sam leaned in and gave Julianne a dry peck on her forehead. "Be happy, child," he muttered.

"I am," she promised, as she caressed his weathered cheek. "Thank you, Sam, for everything."

"It should be Glory and me thanking you. You and Big Luke made us welcome on the trail out here, and now here you are starting fresh."

At that moment, the entrance to the large house was filled with guests all jostling for a position to extend their best wishes to the bridal couple before moving on into the Putnam dining room for an impressive spread of food.

"How come me and Laura have to stay with Miz

Foster tonight?" Luke asked when a quiet had fallen over the room as everyone ate.

"Laura and I," Julianne corrected automatically. "And it's because…" She faltered for the best explanation, looking to Glory for help.

"It's tradition," Glory said. "Now eat your supper or there will be no cake for you, young man."

"But—"

"Come on," Laura said, nudging her brother into the next room. "Let's go sit on the stairs. I'll explain it all to you later."

The rest of the reception went by so fast it was as if Julianne and Nathan were living in a dream. Before they knew it they were being bundled into the Putnam's sleigh. Jacob handed Nathan the reins. "See you tomorrow," he said. He gave the horse a smack on its rump and they were off.

"I like your hat," Julianne said, suddenly shy with her new husband.

"The men gave it to me—a wedding present." He was nervous as well, and that was comforting to his new wife.

She placed her gloved hand on his and he glanced at her and smiled.

By the time they reached their farm, Julianne's head was resting on his shoulder and she had given into the overwhelming exhaustion of an exciting day.

Nathan reined the horse to a stop and kissed her forehead. "You go on in," he said. "I'll unhitch the horse and see to the other animals." He climbed down and came around to lift her to the ground.

They stood for a minute holding each other under the star-filled sky. "I love you, Mrs. Cook."

"Captain, my captain," she whispered and stood on tiptoe to kiss him.

Inside, she stirred the embers of the fire they had left that morning and considered putting on some water for tea, then hearing the whinny of the Putnam's horse, she ran to the window instead. She wanted to see him, to never let him out of her sight. She wanted to remind herself just how blessed she and the children were that this good and gentle man had come into their lives. "Thank you, God," she whispered as she watched him stroke the horse's mane and lead the animal under shelter for the night. "Thank you for all the blessings you have brought to this house."

She had bowed her head and closed her eyes on this last prayer, and when she opened them, she noticed tiny green shoots peeking out of the black earth of several tin cans. She ran to the other window hardly daring to believe her eyes. It was the same there.

She ran to the door and threw it open. "Nathan, we have apple trees," she cried. "Come see." She grabbed his hand and pulled him to the window.

"Well look at that," he said huskily, and closed his eyes for a long moment. When he opened them he took Julianne in his arms and held her, rocking from side to side.

"Come on," he said grabbing a quilt from the bed and wrapping her in it.

"Nathan, it's nearly midnight and it's freezing," she protested, but she was laughing and she followed him willingly.

Outside, he led her to the small grove of apple trees. "Think of it, Julianne. Trees to the horizon and just there…" He pointed to a low rise that protected a part of the land nearest the river. "We'll build our house and raise our children and cradle our grandchildren and—"

"Stop. You're making us old before our time," Julianne protested, but she was holding him, hugging him to her as they dreamed of the future they would share with God's blessing. She looked up and saw the stars lighting the black of the night and she felt a peace she had not known for over a year.

"Thank you," she whispered to the heavens just before Nathan kissed her. Then he scooped her into his arms and continued kissing her all the way back to the little sod house that in that moment she decided they would always keep to remind them of how truly blessed they had been.

* * * * *

Dear Reader,

It always amazes (and inspires) me when I reach a point in the story that calls for some detail that will be unique to the story. I was very troubled by what gift Nathan might choose to give Julianne for Christmas. Then, without even being aware of my writing dilemma, my husband surprised me on Christmas morning with the most beautiful alabaster heart, and a note that is mine to keep and yours to imagine, that made this heart very, very special for me. The next time I sat down to write the scene where Julianne opens the gift Nathan has left her, I had no problem at all knowing what was inside that box. It was his declaration of love—his heart given to her. Whether you are reading this over the holidays or at some other time of the year, I hope you will find the story of Julianne and Nathan's return to faith and love one that touches you and inspires you to remember that opening your heart to others is a sure path to everlasting joy.

All best wishes to you in this season of faith, joy and love.

Anne Schmidt

QUESTIONS FOR DISCUSSION

1. Have you or someone close to you suffered the loss of your first love, and if so, what are your memories of the journey that followed that loss?

2. How would you answer someone who had suffered a tragedy and asked you how God could let such a thing happen?

3. What role does faith play in Julianne's reaction to the death of her husband, Luke? How does that role change by the end of the story?

4. In many ways, the homesteaders who formed the community of Homestead are extended family for one another. What makes the bond they share so unique?

5. When Nathan chooses marrying Julianne over going to California to reunite with his brother, do you think he made the right choice? Why, or why not?

6. Is Julianne making the right choice in insisting that she secure the land for her children, or is she simply being stubborn? What are your reasons for choosing one decision over the other?

7. Think about an issue you may be wrestling with in your life, and consider whether or not there are ways that God is guiding you in a certain direction.

A COWBOY'S
CHRISTMAS
Linda Ford

Christmas is a favorite holiday made all the more special by family gatherings. This book is dedicated to my family. Without you my Christmas celebration would be dull and uneventful. Thanks to each one of you for making my life full, busy and joyful. I love you.

For God so loved the world that he gave his one and only Son, that whoever believes in him shall not perish but have eternal life.

—*John* 3:16

Chapter One

1888 Canadian Rockies

A murmur of voices warned eighteen-year-old Winnie Lockwood she'd overslept. Hay tickled her nose and throat. Cold touched her back where the hay had shifted away leaving her exposed.

Exposed! If she was discovered...

She wiggled, but her movement made so much noise she drew in her breath and held it, praying she hadn't been noticed. She cupped her hand to her nose and mouth, forcing back a cough from the dust. The hay had been fragrant and welcoming last night, when she'd sought refuge and warmth. Today she was aware of the musty scent and imagined bugs creeping along her skin. It took every ounce of self-control to keep from squirming.

"I'll fork up feed for the animals," a male voice called.

Was it friendly? Harsh? Dangerous?

One thing Winnie had learned was, you could never be certain what lay beneath the surface of a voice or a face. A kind face readily enough disguised a mean spirit and kind words often enough proved false.

"We need to head for town in good time."

The voice had grown perilously close. She could almost feel the tines of a feed fork pierce her skin, and she bolted upright, gaining her feet in a flurry of hay. She sneezed and swiped her hands over her very untidy coat.

"Who are you? What are you doing in my barn?"

The masculine voice had deepened several degrees and carried a clear warning.

Holding her arms out in a gesture she hoped indicated she meant no harm and had no weapon, she faced the man. Not much older than she, his chin jutted out in a challenging way. Knowing her life depended on a quick evaluation, she took in his dark eyes, the way he'd pulled his Stetson low, how he balanced on the balls of his feet, the pitch fork at ready for defense. A man who would not give an inch, who would tolerate no nonsense. The thought both frightened and appealed.

"I mean no harm. Just looking for a place out of the cold. I'll be on my way now." She glanced toward the door and escape, and made as if to lower her arms, testing his reaction.

"Now hang on. How am I to know you didn't steal something?"

She grinned openly. "Don't hardly see how I'd fit a horse or even a saddle under my coat."

A deep chuckle came from behind the man. "Think she's got a point." An older man, with a grizzled, three-day growth of beard and eyes flashing with amusement, stepped closer. "Seems you should be a little more concerned with why a pretty young woman is sleeping in your barn, than whether or not she might hide a horse beneath her coat."

The younger man grunted. "More likely she's a front for something else." He shook the fork threateningly. "How many others are there?"

Winnie wiggled her hands. "I'm alone."

"Head for the door and no sudden moves." He waved the fork again and she decided she didn't want to question his sincerity in using it.

"I tell you, I only wanted someplace to get out of the wind." She was on her way to Banff and a job at the sanitorium, but had run out of funds at Long Valley and started walking, hoping to arrive under her own steam or get a ride. Instead, darkness and cold had found her searching for a place to spend the night. She'd planned to slip into the barn for a few hours and be gone again before anyone discovered her.

"Now, Derek—" The older man sounded placating. "Don't be hasty."

"Hasty? Kathy is alone in the house. If your accomplices have—" He indicated she should move.

"My bag."

"Uncle Mac, grab that."

Winnie edged across the expanse to draw the door open and stepped outside, breathing deeply of the fresh air. The day was sunny with a promise of warmth later on. A welcome change from the cold wind of last night that threatened snow and drove her to sleep in the barn of this man. At least there was a Kathy. That gave her hope for a little generosity that would let her get on her way without any more complications.

Sensing the man would not take kindly to her bolting for freedom, and knowing she'd never outrun him, she marched toward the simple ranch house, one-story with a verandah across the side. Welcoming enough under normal circumstances. She kicked the dust from her shoes before she stepped to the wooden floor of the verandah.

"Wait right there." It was the man called Derek. "Your friends have any sort of firearm?"

"I told you—"

"Answer the question." He nudged her with the tines of the fork. They didn't pierce her coat, but she jerked away, not caring to tempt him to push a little harder.

"Now, son, don't be doing anything rash."

"Uncle Mac, I am not prepared to take any chances. Especially when it comes to Kathy's safety." His voice grew gravely, as if Kathy meant more than anything else to him. Seems he was a man who cared deeply. Something quivered in the pit of Winnie's stomach—a familiar, forbidden feeling rolled up in denial. She tried to force anger into that place to quench it but failed miserably. Something in the way this man was prepared to fight assailants, numbers and strength unknown, poured emptiness into her soul. She pushed aside the foolishness. She was headed for Banff and a job. She wanted nothing more.

"I understand that." The older man, Uncle Mac, edged forward. "Why don't I have a look?"

"Be careful. I don't trust her."

Winnie snorted. "Who'd have guessed it?"

Uncle Mac shot her an amused look that fled in an instant when Derek made a discouraging sound. The older man edged forward, slowly opened the door and peeked around. "Don't see nothing."

Winnie bit back a foolish desire to ask if they lived in an unfurnished house.

"Do you see Kathy?

"Nope. Nothing."

"Go in slow and easy. We'll be right behind you. And I warn you, miss, don't make a sound to alert your friends or I'll be forced to jab this fork in up to its hilt."

Uncle Mac drew his head back and glanced over his shoulder. "You'll do no such thing." Without waiting for Derek's reply he slipped into the house.

Winnie followed. She'd laugh at all this unnecessary drama except she wasn't sure what Derek's reaction would be and he did carry a sharp pitchfork with long tines.

As if to reinforce her doubts, he murmured, "Don't think I'm a softy like Uncle Mac."

"Oh, no, sir. I surely wouldn't make that mistake."

She tried her hardest to keep the amusement from her voice but wondered if she'd succeeded. What would it be like to have a man as ready to defend her as Derek was to defend Kathy? Aching swelled in a spot behind her eyes.

She stepped into the room. A big farm kitchen with evidence of lots of living. Messy enough to be welcoming...for the people who belonged here.

"Check her bedroom."

Uncle Mac tiptoed through a doorway.

Winnie grinned, grateful the man behind her couldn't guess how much enjoyment she got from all this.

Uncle Mac returned, a little girl at his side. Winnie put her at about nine or ten.

"She was playing on her bed. As blissful as a lamb." He ruffled the child's already untidy hair.

This must be Kathy.

Winnie studied the girl. Brown hair, beautiful brown eyes, with the innocence of childhood tarnished. Where was the mother? Which of these men was the father?

The child's eyes widened with curiosity when she saw Winnie. "Who's that?" She bent sideways to see Derek. "How come you got a fork pushed into her back, huh, Derek?"

Guess that meant Uncle Mac was the father.

Derek parked the fork by the door. "So you *are* alone?"

Alone? In more ways than he could imagine. "Just like I said."

"About time we showed some hospitality." Uncle Mac

headed for the stove. "Kathy, set the table for four and we'll have breakfast."

Winnie's stomach growled in anticipation. She pretended she didn't notice.

Kathy giggled.

"Kat." Derek warned. "Your manners." His voice was as gentle as summer dew. Winnie blinked as the ache behind her eyeballs grew larger, more intense.

The child scurried to put out four plates, and Uncle Mac broke a stack of eggs into a fry pan.

Winnie followed every movement of his hands. She hoped she'd be allowed a generous portion of those eggs. She'd eaten only once yesterday, and heaven alone knew where she'd get the next meal after she left here. *Lord, you know my need. Provide as You have promised.*

"Sit," Uncle Mac nodded toward a chair. "Tell us your name."

Winnie gave it as she moved the stack of socks and mittens to the floor and sat. Her mouth flooded with saliva like a river suddenly thawed. Her plate had a rim of grease but she didn't wipe it off. She'd have eaten off the table if she had to. Or the floor for that matter.

"I'm Mac Adams. You've met my nephew, Derek. This is my niece, Kathy." His expression softened as he turned to the girl.

Winnie nodded a gracious hello.

Uncle Mac scooped generous piles of eggs to three plates and a tiny portion to Kathy's. He sat at Winnie's right. "Shall we give thanks?"

Grateful for the food and the temporary reprieve,

Winnie silently poured out her thanks as Uncle Mac spoke his aloud.

"Amen," he said.

"Amen," Winnie echoed with heartfelt sincerity.

Kathy giggled.

Derek cleared his throat, his warning glance full of affection, and Kathy ducked her head over her breakfast.

Winnie pushed away the longing that threatened to unhitch a wagonload of tears. She only wanted to be on her way to Banff. Winnie forced herself to eat slowly, ladylike.

Uncle Mac picked up the dishes as soon as he was certain she was finished, and added them to the stack on the cupboard by the stove. "Now, young lady, let's hear why you're alone and spending the night in a barn."

She'd known this question was coming, but still hadn't figured out an answer. Her conscience wouldn't allow her to lie. But neither would she tell the whole truth. "Got lost."

"From who and from where?" Derek's question was far more demanding.

"I thought I was on the main road. Obviously I was wrong." She pushed her chair back. "Thank you for the food. Much appreciated. Let me clean up the dishes in exchange, then I'll head back to town."

"No need," Derek protested. "We can manage without help."

Kathy leaned forward, her expression eager. "I don't mind if she helps."

At the same time, Uncle Mac said, "If it's a ride to town you're needing, we'll take you when we go."

They all ground to a halt and tried to sort their conversations out.

Winnie chuckled. "I'll be happy to do the dishes and I'd welcome a ride to town."

Derek looked ready to protest, but Kathy bounced from the table and Uncle Mac slapped his thighs. "It's settled then."

Derek got to his feet so fast Winnie wondered if something had bitten him. "You two stay here while I finish chores and get the wagon ready."

"I'll be along," Uncle Mac said.

"Stay here." He paused halfway across the room and muttered, "No way I'm leaving Kathy alone with her." The door banged shut after him, then swung open again and he grabbed the fork. The slap of the second closing echoed through the room.

And reverberated in Winnie's heart, striking at the feelings she struggled so hard to deny. To have someone who cared that much was a dream beyond her reach.

Winnie pushed to her feet and tackled the stack of dishes, using water hot enough to dissolve the buildup of grease and redden her hands.

Uncle Mac wandered out of the room, leaving her alone with Kathy. She handed the child a drying towel.

Kathy's chin jutted out. Her eyes flashed all sorts of emotions.

She'd try to sidetrack the child. "Shouldn't you be in school?"

Kathy lifted her head. "I get to miss school today because we're going to get my new nanny."

"I see. What happened to your last one?"

"She got married." Tears welled up. "Why couldn't she be happy with us? Now I got to get used to someone else. I hate it. They always have new rules. It makes me sad and mad all at the same time."

Sad and angry explained perfectly the way Winnie felt most of her life. A bitter tenderness touched a place in her heart, that this child should experience the same pain. She closed her eyes and steeled away the gall in her throat, the churn in her chest. As soon as they were under control she concentrated on the girl at her side. *Lord, help me say something to help her before I depart.* "I've felt that way many times. It's pretty confusing."

Tears glittered in Kathy's eyes as she nodded.

Winnie dropped her hand to a thin shoulder, felt the child tense but didn't remove her hand. "It sometimes seems the feelings are eating up your insides, doesn't it?"

Kathy choked back a sob.

"Kathy, it's alright to feel sad. People come and go. Things change. Nothing stays the same except who you are in here." She touched the child's chest. "Nothing can take that away from you. One thing that helps me when I'm feeling bad is to remember God loves me. He holds me in His hands. I am never alone."

"I just want someone with arms to love me."

"I know." Oh, how she knew. But she'd outgrown the need. Now all she wanted was a job, a place to keep warm and no reason to expect more than room and wages. "You have Derek and your Uncle Mac." Uncle Mac seemed kindly and gentle; Derek, an appealing combination of tough and tender. She tried to stifle a longing for devotion like she'd witnessed. She wrenched her thoughts back into order. Not only did she know nothing about Derek, she knew enough not to seek after things unavailable to her.

"I miss my mama." Tears flowed unchecked, leaving a dirty streak on Kathy's face.

Winnie flung about in her thoughts for an answer. Something to help this child deal with her situation. For a heartbeat, she imagined staying for a time and teaching Kathy ways to deal with her sorrow. But she was done working for families. Wanting to belong. Knowing she didn't. Even when she thought she had reason to believe otherwise. "Honey, where's your mama?"

"In heaven. She died in an accident. She and Peter and Susan. Only I didn't. And 'course, Derek, but he wasn't with us."

She guessed that made Derek Kathy's brother. "I'm so sorry. I expect your mama loved you."

"Lots and lots."

"And I expect she liked to see you happy."

Kathy's tears stopped and she smiled. "Mama used to tickle me just to hear me laugh, she said."

"So if your mama could hear you, she'd want most to hear you laugh, I suppose."

Kathy nodded.

"What if she *can* hear you?"

Kathy shook her head. "She's in heaven with Papa. But I don't remember Papa."

"Jesus can hear you."

Kathy waited for her to continue, her eyes wide with consideration.

"I expect He can tell your mama if you laugh or don't." She wasn't sure if people in heaven saw their loved ones on earth or not, but of course Jesus could. She had no qualms about assuring Kathy that.

"I guess so all right." Kathy seemed intrigued by the idea.

"So, even though it's all right to be sad and angry once in a while, don't forget to laugh for your mama."

Kathy brightened. "I won't."

Winnie finished washing the dishes, then poured boiling water on the table and set to scrubbing it.

By the time Derek returned the kitchen was clean, the dishpan hung behind the stove, the towels draped over hooks to dry.

Kathy played with a well-worn stuffed doll.

"Uncle Mac," Derek roared. "Where are you?"

The older man clattered into the room, smoothing his hair.

"You were sleeping? Who was watching Kathy?"

"She was," Kathy jabbed her finger toward Winnie.

Derek's frown deepened, giving his face harsh angles and making his eyes dark and unfriendly. "Kathy, get your coat. We're going to town." The look he favored

Winnie with left no doubt. They couldn't wait to get rid of her.

Winnie mentally shrugged as she donned her dusty coat and waited for the others. She was equally anxious to resume her journey. She would not acknowledge the hollowness just behind her breastbone that never quite went away. A longing for home and love—her gaze darted to Derek, who smiled at Kathy, a look on his face as full of affection as any she had imagined. A man who loved openly and freely. Her heart hovering over a deep chasm of emptiness, Winnie jerked away to stare at the door.

The woman—Winnie—was behind him. Uncle Mac shared the back bench. Derek had made sure Kathy sat beside him on the front seat where he could guard her. This little mite of a girl was all he had left of his family. He would never let anything harm her. At twenty-three, he was simultaneously orphaned and thrust into the role of both mother and father to his little sister. A role he did not object to except for the reason for it.

Getting Winnie back to town as soon as possible would ease his mind regarding Kathy's safety. What kind of woman wandered about the country alone and slept in barns? Certainly not the kind he wanted Kathy associating with. He grinned as he recalled Winnie crawling out of the feed, all dusty and dotted with flecks of hay. His heart had missed a beat at how easily he might have jabbed his fork into her. Even in her disarray she was appealing—eyes like strong coffee and every bit as jolting, hair like mink fur.

He flattened his grin. He had no room in his heart or life for pretty gals, no matter how fiery her eyes, how spunky her attitude.

"Fortunate we don't have snow yet," Uncle Mac mused. "Sometimes it's up to the horses' bellies this late in the year."

Derek guessed he meant the latter for Winnie, because it was not news to Derek.

"The mountains are pretty with their snowcap," Winnie said. "Like a glittering necklace."

Kathy giggled. "For a giant."

Derek shifted on the seat and kept silent. Maybe if he didn't add to the conversation, it would end and allow him to settle into businesslike thoughts.

For a few minutes, the soft plod of the horses' hooves on the packed trail was the only sound.

He relaxed and glanced about. The deciduous trees were bare-limbed. The pine and spruce were dark winter green. Yes, they often had snow by now. It was the end of November, after all.

Not a good time to be bringing in a new housekeeper, though he'd discovered there was no such thing as a good time. Why did Miss Agnew have to pick early winter to pack up and leave? Couldn't she put off her wedding until spring? Or at least until after Christmas? Her leaving would make the season even more difficult for Kathy. And she already had enough trouble with missing their mother and sister and brother. He clenched his hand on the reins. His jaw tightened. He should have never let them travel alone. If he'd been with them, he might have prevented the accident, though a train wreck was beyond his control.

Not beyond God's, though, and yet He'd done nothing. Sure made it hard to trust God to take care of them.

Kathy's clear voice sang, "I sing the mighty power of God, that made the mountains rise."

Lonesomeness as endless as train tracks gripped him. It had been their mother's favorite song. She sang it as she washed dishes, as she weeded the garden and as she mended. "Where did you hear that song?"

"Mama used to sing it all the time."

His heart clenched like an angry fist. All Kathy had were memories of their mother. She deserved more. A mother to hug her and kiss her and tuck her into bed at night. He could never replace their mother, and the housekeepers he'd hired only looked on Kathy's care as a job, and moved on as soon as they found a man, which didn't take long out here, where men greatly outnumbered women. "I didn't think you'd remember."

"Yup."

Why was she singing it now? And without tears and sobbing.

Kathy paused. "I think Mama likes to hear me sing. She—" Kathy nodded toward Winnie "—said Mama would like to see me happy."

Derek turned right around to stare at the woman behind him.

She smiled sweetly, her eyes sparking with what he

took to be a combination of amusement and challenge. "I'm sure you agree."

His thoughts were a hopeless tangle of memories of his ma. Surprise, pleasure and sadness at hearing Kathy sing their mother's favorite song.

And something nameless, inviting and challenging in Winnie's gaze. He snapped a lid closed on mental wanderings and jerked back to look at Kathy, who regarded him with wide-eyed innocence. "I think Mama would like it very much."

Kathy faced forward and continued to sing.

"I don't know what you said," Uncle Mac murmured, his voice sliding below the sound of Kathy's cheery voice. "But it certainly made a good impression on our Kathy. Thank you."

"I like the song she's singing. Doesn't it give you hope?"

Seemingly unaware of the conversation, Kathy continued. "I sing the goodness of the Lord."

Derek wondered how to rejoice in the goodness of the Lord when it seemed life was so often out of control. But he said nothing. They topped the hill and looked down at Long Valley.

The town had been named for obvious reasons. It lay in a fertile valley between high hills, with the Rockies rising to the west. The Deer River flowed at the feet of the town. It was now iced over though he knew better than to think the ice was solid enough to hold a horse. The weather had been too uncertain.

They rattled down the hill on the road that became

the main street. Wood-framed buildings housed businesses of every sort. "Where shall I let you off?" He directed his question to Winnie.

"Wherever you're stopping is fine for me."

He turned toward the rail station.

Kathy fell silent and sat up straight. Her face lost the gentleness and joy she'd revealed while singing, replaced with tightness about her eyes. White circled her lips signaling her tension.

"It's okay, Kit Kat." He squeezed her hands. "I'm getting a married couple. The man is going to work for us, too, so they won't be leaving any time soon."

Young Eric, who helped his father run the station, trotted from the building. "Hey, good to see you, Derek. Saves me a trip to your place with this here telegram." He waved the sheet of yellow paper.

Uncle Mac, who'd been about to jump down and assist their guest to the ground, stopped and waited.

Kathy whimpered.

"No need to get upset," he murmured, but of course she knew a telegram always brought bad news.

No one moved as Eric jogged over to hand Derek the slip of paper. Even Winnie seemed to have forgotten she meant to get off here. Was she aware of the tension in the others? Did it make her limbs as weak as it did his? He dismissed the idea. Of course it didn't. She had no interest in what happened to this family.

He gave the boy a few coins and Eric trotted back to the station. Derek unfolded the page and silently read the words.

Chapter Two

"Who is it from?" Uncle Mac demanded. "What does it say?"

"It's from the Faringtons."

"Weren't they supposed to be here?"

He expected them to arrive to help with Kathy. "They aren't coming until after Christmas. Got a new grand-baby to visit." He crumpled the page and stuffed it into his pocket. Now what was he supposed to do? He didn't like leaving Kathy alone while they worked outside.

"No one wants to take care of me." Kathy's words caught on a sob.

"That's not true. I do."

"You're too busy. 'Sides you're a man." She sucked in a gulp of air and released it in a wail.

Being a man certainly inconvenienced him at times, but he couldn't change that. Kathy's crying intensified.

Eric reappeared in the baggage room doorway, his

eyes wide with curiosity. His father stuck his head out the wicket window to see what the racket was.

"Hush, Kathy." Derek tried to pull her to his lap.

She shoved him away.

Uncle Mac tried. She pushed him away, too.

"Winnie, what are your plans?" Uncle Mac asked. "You and Kathy got along real well. Perhaps you could stay until these other people arrive."

Derek's nerves jerked. No way would they ask her to stay. Something about her made thinking clearly difficult. He shot Uncle Mac a hard look, but before he could protest, Winnie spoke.

"I'm on my way to Banff."

"What's in Banff?" Uncle Mac seemed set on seeing Winnie as a suitable stand-in for the Faringtons.

"Uncle Mac—"

Again, Winnie spoke before Derek could voice his protests. "The Banff Sanitorium, where people go for the healing waters. Friends of my former employer said it was a lovely place. They are always in need of quality staff."

And she considered herself such? Flecks of hay spattered her coat. Her hair needed a good brushing. And yet, his kitchen had shone after her short visit, and for a few minutes, Kathy had been happier than he'd seen her since the accident. And that was a year and a half ago.

"Can't the sanitorium wait?" Uncle Mac persisted. "We'd pay you as much as you'd make there."

"She don't want to stay with me. No one does." Kathy's cries grew louder.

Winnie leaned forward and touched Kathy's shoulder. "I'd like to take care of you. In fact, I can't think of anything I'd rather do."

Kathy choked off a sob and spun around. "Would you?"

Whoa. All Derek knew about this young woman was she slept in barns at night. That didn't recommend her in his mind, even if she had a reassuring way of calming Kathy. Her presence had the opposite effect on him, leaving him fighting confusion. "Kathy, I don't think—"

She folded into a sobbing heap.

"Derek, it seems you don't have a lot of options."

He flung his uncle an angry look. "We know nothing about her."

"So ask me. I'm right here."

He and his uncle silently challenged each other. Reluctantly, Derek gave in. He edged the wagon away from the station and far enough from the town so they could talk in semi-privacy and no one would stare at them, wondering why Kathy was acting up this time. He shifted around to face Winnie. "Where is your family?"

She shrugged.

"They kick you out?" Had she done something so dreadful they'd disowned her. Though the idea of doing so scraped along his nerves.

"I've been working for some people, but they didn't need me any longer."

"Why?"

"A cousin came west to join them. She took my place."

"Who are these people?"

"I doubt you know them."

At his demanding look, she continued. "The Krauses from Saskatoon. Reginald and Moira."

"You're right. I never heard of them." No way was he going to entrust his little sister to a stranger with no one to say whether or not she was suitable.

Uncle Mac leaned forward. "Seems it would be simple enough to wire these folks."

"Of course." He turned the wagon toward town.

Kathy's sobs subsided. "She's going to stay?"

"Don't get your hopes up. First thing I'm going to do is send off a telegram. Then we'll wait until we hear back."

At the station, Winnie provided him with the address of the Krauses and he sent the message. "Now we wait for a reply. Kathy, maybe you should go to school."

"No." Her chin quivered. "Don't make me. I have to know if Winnie is staying."

He didn't blame her for not wanting to sit at school worrying about things. "Just for today then."

She twisted the edge of her coat so hard he knew it would end up torn, but he couldn't bring himself to tell her to stop. And the way she worried her lip on her teeth warned him she would have a sore before the day was out.

If only he could provide her with the security she needed and deserved. The Faringtons were meant to help provide that. An older couple eager to stay in one place. At least they wouldn't be rushing off to marry, as all the others had done.

They went to the mercantile. "I'll buy you a penny candy," he told Kathy, hoping to cheer her up.

"Come along." Uncle Mac jumped down and held his hand out to help Winnie. "Buy whatever you need while you're here. No telling when we'll get to town again if winter sets in."

"Thank you." She wandered over to the ladies section.

Derek took Kathy to the counter and they spent fifteen minutes making a selection. She finally selected a red-and-white-striped candy stick. He bought himself a handful of lemon drops and stashed them in his pocket for a time when he craved their sweetness.

Uncle Mac reminded him of supplies they needed, and they waited for their order to be filled. Several times, he glanced at Winnie, but she continued to examine items without making a selection. After a bit, it dawned on him that she likely had no funds. That might provide one explanation as to why she was sleeping in his barn. Lost. No money. No family. Something inside him edged sideways at the thought. He knew the pain of losing family. At least he had Kathy and Uncle Mac. And he intended to do all in his power to protect them.

He wanted to go home, but not until he'd given Mr. Krause a chance to get the telegram and reply. If the man was in his office, a response would take only a few hours. No point in making Eric ride all the way out to the ranch. He turned to Kathy. "What do you say to going over to the hotel for tea?"

Kathy's eyes brightened. "Could we?"

The seldom-indulged-in treat would help pass the time. He signaled to Winnie. Uncle Mac stepped to her side to escort her. Derek clamped down on his teeth as he took Kathy's hand. Let Uncle Mac walk at Winnie's side. Derek didn't care.

Only he *did*. Admitting so scalded his innards.

They spent a tense hour at the hotel, trying to enjoy the tea and selection of baked goodies. Uncle Mac seemed the only one who succeeded. Derek wondered what he was doing, considering asking a young woman to stay, who in a matter of hours had proven such an upset to his thoughts.

Eric strode through the door. "Telegram, Derek."

He read the few words. "Winnifred Lockwood excellent worker. Stop. Honest. Stop. Trustworthy. Stop. Cheerful. Stop. Wouldn't hesitate to recommend her to you. Stop. Reginald Krause."

Derek wondered why they had let such a paragon of virtue leave.

Winnie wouldn't look at Derek, wouldn't try and guess what the telegram contained. She'd worked hard at the Krauses, but her best efforts had failed to provide her with permanency. She shifted her mind back to the store where she'd admired some fine wool fabric. The burnt-red with tiny yellow flowers would make a lovely dress. Not that she'd ever have such. Her wardrobe consisted of the dress she wore plus one other, both given to her out of the charity of Mrs. Krause's sister. At the sanitorium they provided uniforms. She welcomed the idea. A uniform would give her a bit of anonymity—a young woman doing her job. No need to feel anything toward the patients and visitors except kindness. She would not allow herself to feel more. Doing so in the past caused her nothing but sadness and anger. She had to move on.

Yet she'd agreed to stay with Kathy for a month.

Only because the money would enable her to complete her journey and arrive in Banff looking like more than a vagabond.

"What does it say?" Kathy demanded.

Derek handed the note to Uncle Mac, then turned and pinned Winnie into immobility with his dark eyes. "Seems we would be fortunate to have you work for us."

She swallowed hard, unable to think how she should respond.

"Bear in mind it will be temporary. Only until Christmas, when the Faringtons will arrive.

"I understand, and it suits me fine." This time she would not let herself care about any of them. She'd treat them kindly, of course. She could do no less.

Derek signaled to the others. "She'll be coming home with us. Only until the Faringtons arrive," he warned Kathy.

Disappointment filled Kathy's eyes.

Winnie wished she could assure the child otherwise, but she couldn't. She eyed Derek from under the cover of her eyelashes. Why didn't he marry and provide a permanent arrangement for them all?

She pulled her chin in and faced ahead. Perhaps he had a wife already picked out. After all, he was an attractive man with appealing qualities, such as devotion to his family, readiness to defend and...

She sat up straighter and forced her thoughts into submission. It mattered not one way or another to her. She'd only be here until Christmas.

She ignored the sorrow and anger flooding her soul. There was only one thing she had control over, and that was her spirit; and she had vowed a long time ago that she would not allow a root of bitterness to spring up.

On the way back, Winnie's lungs felt stiff, as if they had forgotten their task was to take air in and out. What had she done? She'd promised herself not to get involved with another family, yet here she was, riding to the ranch with Uncle Mac at her side, Kathy and Derek in front of her. Kathy kept up a steady stream of chatter, but Uncle Mac was the only one who answered. For the life of her, Winnie couldn't manage a sensible thought. Over and over she mentally chanted, *it's only to help Kathy. Nothing more. There's nothing for me here. Nothing at all.*

She almost succeeded in not allowing herself to study Derek's back. Ramrod straight. A rock to his family.

Back at the house, Derek let them off. "Show her the housekeeper's quarters. I'll put the horses away."

Uncle Mac led the way to the room off the kitchen behind the stove, Kathy bouncing along at his side. "I hope you'll find it comfortable," Uncle Mac said, as he put her bag on the bed.

Besides the bed that was big enough for a couple, the room held a dresser and a mirror. The window looked out toward the mountains. "I'm sure I shall."

"We'll give you time to get settled. Come on, Kit Kat."

Kathy paused at the doorway. "I'm glad you're going to stay."

Winnie pushed aside her doubts and smiled at Kathy. "Thank you."

A few minutes later she returned to the kitchen and took over her temporary duties.

Soup simmered on the stove as Derek stepped indoors. Their gazes locked across the room, hers wary, his more than a little annoyed, as if he resented that he had been forced to ask her to stay. She narrowed her eyes. She'd agreed only for Kathy's sake.

But a frisson of tension hovered about her as she served the meal and later cleaned the kitchen. She felt Derek's presence, his watchfulness, even when he wasn't watching her.

To escape the uneasiness she went to her room early.

Three days later she had settled into a routine after a serious talk with herself. This house had everything she wanted and nothing she could have. She had only to accept the fact. Life became easier once she did.

Kathy had returned to school. Derek spent much of his time outside, likely in the barn. Either because of work or to avoid Winnie. Uncle Mac had long naps, then joined Derek. Mornings and evenings were easiest with Kathy present.

Except for one thing. Kathy did not go to sleep easily.

Tonight she cried in Derek's arms as he rocked her, trying to soothe her.

She finally fell asleep, remnants of her sobs shuddering through her. Derek rocked her a few more minutes, then eased from the chair and tiptoed into her bedroom.

Winnie turned from the window where she'd tried to take her thoughts to the silvery moonlight in hopes of ignoring Kathy's distress. She plunked to a chair and let her head fall forward. Her intention had been so simple three days ago—a month of keeping house, seeing Kathy to school and making meals. Nothing more. No emotional connection.

But life never turned out exactly as she planned.

Bedtime was torture for Kathy. She couldn't bear to be alone in the dark. A lamp didn't help. After a few minutes of listening to her sobs, Derek went to her and spent upwards of an hour rocking her, assuring her he was right there and would always be.

Trouble was, all of them knew he couldn't promise forever.

Life was too uncertain.

Winnie had learned that truth at a young age. So had Kathy.

Going to school was equally painful. "How do I know you won't all be gone when I get back?" Tears streamed down Kathy's face.

Winnie had stood aside and let Derek and Uncle Mac deal with Kathy. After all, they were family. They would be here long after Winnie left.

But neither of the men seemed to know how to calm her fears, and the strain on all of them was obvious.

When Kathy started crying tonight, Mac had mumbled something about seeing to the stock and then headed for the barn.

They all knew he was escaping Kathy's distress.

Derek stepped back into the room, deep lines gouged around his mouth, dark misery in his eyes. She'd seen the same distress every bedtime and every morning when Kathy headed down the road to the little schoolhouse on the corner, Derek at her side.

She now knew enough to have a pot of tea ready when Kathy finally went to sleep.

She poured him a cup and edged the sugar bowl closer.

Derek spooned sugar into his tea. At the fourth

spoonful, she knew he wasn't aware of what he did and she pushed the bowl away. He stirred his tea. Round and round and round, the spoon tinkling on the china with a cheerless tolling.

"She's been like this since the accident."

Winnie nodded, though he didn't look at her. "She told me her mama and a sister and brother died."

"In a train wreck on their way out here." His voice was harsh. "I was supposed to be with them, but I decided at the last minute to let them travel alone."

She murmured a sound she hoped indicated she heard. If he needed to talk she would listen. She could do that much without getting involved with this family's distress—without letting her emotions crawl up her throat and reach out to Derek.

Then she would go to Banff. A uniform. A job. A room. All she wanted or needed.

"I should have been with them."

Shock jolted through her veins. Did he mean he wished he'd died? "Good thing you weren't. Otherwise, who would take care of Kathy?"

"How can I hope to protect her? Life just happens."

"Life is in God's hands."

He jerked up to face her. "I suppose your life has fit into neat little slots, so it's easy for you to say that."

She laughed. "Yes, that would explain why I was sleeping in your barn."

He looked a little uncertain.

She couldn't resist the urge to further upset his idea of

how easy her life was. "I know more about how Kathy is feeling than you could ever believe."

"Huh?"

He doubted her, did he? Well, she would soon enough convince him. "When I was seven, my parents gave me to my aunt and uncle and moved west with no forwarding address."

He looked suitably shocked. Or was he perhaps disbelieving?

"My aunt and uncle were childless and my parents had seven children."

"So you ended up in a better home?"

"One might think so, except my aunt then had two children." After their own children arrived, her aunt and uncle had used Winnie as a servant. She'd moved to an attic room and ran errands from dawn to dusk. She'd done so willingly, eagerly, certain she would earn affection and approval. "My aunt died giving birth to a third who didn't live." Her security had died with her. "My uncle married a young neighborhood woman within a few months, and the new wife wanted nothing to do with a child that belonged to neither of them. At twelve, I was hired out to the Anderson family." She tried to keep her voice light. As if it didn't still hurt.

"How did you come to be working for the Krauses?" No doubt he still thought she was fabricating all the details.

"After four years with the Andersons, they decided they didn't need me anymore." So much for all the talk about how valuable she was. Just like a member of the family. "I was hired by the Krauses then."

"How long were you with them?"

"Two years." She clamped her mouth shut. She would say nothing further. When she went to the Krauses she'd promised herself there would be no more dreams of belonging. She'd do her job well. Give them no reason to dismiss her. But she would be content to be a servant.

Only, Moira and Reginald had invited her to take part in family activities, taken her on family vacations. Given her hope. Fueled her dreams.

She'd been so foolish to think she could belong. All it had taken was a letter from a cousin in Germany saying she wanted to visit, perhaps relocate to the Canadian west, and Winnie had been told her services were no longer needed.

Derek touched the back of her hand. "I'm sorry."

She jerked away, her heart thudding against her ribcage like an overwound clock. "I don't need your pity. I welcome the chance to be able to work in Banff. I hear it's a beautiful place."

He dropped his hand to his lap and looked past her. "I heard that, too."

A thick silence hung between them. She pushed her chair back, intending to excuse herself and go to her room.

"Perhaps you do understand how she feels. I share her sorrow but I don't know how to help her."

Winnie shrugged. "Everyone handles trials in their own way."

Derek's gaze bore into hers, dark, challenging, maybe more. Maybe seeking. "How do you deal with yours?"

A great vacuum sucked at her insides. She tried to pull her gaze away, couldn't. "That's easy. I trust myself to God's care. He will never leave me nor forsake me. He holds me in the palm of His hands."

His mouth pulled down at the corners. "My mama believed the same thing and look what happened to her." His breath whooshed out. "And despite your trust in God, you spend the night sleeping in a barn. How can you say He is taking care of you?"

She chuckled softly. "Well, I wasn't asleep in the barn of a cruel man, so I suppose He was watching over me." Had God sent her here for a purpose? To help Kathy. What could she do in a month?

Could she risk her heart becoming involved?

The wind sighed about the house as she considered her answer. An alternative sprang to her mind. Something she'd wondered about a few times. "Why don't you get married? Surely, that would give Kathy security."

He jerked to his feet, his fists curled on the table top. "I have no intention of marrying. Ever."

"I can tell you have mixed feelings."

He stared at her then laughed. "Sorry. I was a bit vehement, wasn't I?"

"I barely noticed. But tell me, why are you so set against marriage?"

He settled back to his chair. "I have Kathy to care for. That's my focus."

"Seems to me marriage would make that easier."

His mouth tightened. He shook his head. "I don't need another person to take care of. To worry about. To always know I couldn't protect them as I ought."

"You feel responsible for your mother's death?"

"Wouldn't you, in my shoes?"

She lifted one shoulder. "I have no idea how I'd feel."

"My father died when I was seventeen, after years of illness. His parting words were to take care of the family. I failed completely."

She wanted to comfort him. Give him something to encourage him. Her heart stalled at crossing a boundary she had created to protect herself from growing too close to people.

Quivering with reluctance, she slipped her hand over to rest on the back of his.

He stiffened but didn't pull away.

"You only fail when you don't care."

His eyes darkened enough to match the night outside the window. His gaze searched hers.

She didn't know what he sought, only knew she couldn't provide it. This time she would not let her heart open up to the people of this home. This was a job. Nothing more.

"I care." His voice thickened with emotion.

"I know you do." Despite her best resolve, she ached to experience such caring on her behalf. Determinedly, she pushed aside the yearning, refused to acknowledge it. "So you haven't failed."

He turned his hand and squeezed hers. "Thank you for saying so."

The air between them shimmered with promise. Hope. Unfulfilled dreams. A wish for things to change that could not change, a desire to go back to happier times, happier places. Or better yet, find new happiness. Her heart flooded with sadness as wide as the sky. She scrubbed her lips together and tried to stifle the ache threatening to suck her inside out. Her hand squeezed Derek's without her permission. She tried to pull away. Couldn't make her arm obey. Something deep, gut level, bound her to him.

Chapter Three

Derek blinked, realized he clung to Winnie's hand and pulled away. "Thanks for the tea." And more. Her understanding. The comfort of her touch.

He jerked to his feet. He needed neither. He turned toward the hall, heading for his room. "I'll say good night."

Why had he let himself be drawn into her words? Why had he gripped her hand like Kathy did his on the way to school? He wasn't a frightened child. He needed no one. Wanted no one. Kathy was his responsibility, and he feared he couldn't live up to that adequately. He sat on the edge of his bed and looked at the calendar. December third. The Faringtons would arrive the twenty-seventh. Until then, they had to make do with Winnie's help.

She'd proven herself capable enough at housework. But he didn't need her comfort or words of encouragement.

It sure beat him, how she could believe God was in control when she'd been shoved from pillar to post. He clenched his fists, gritted his teeth. Why did life have to be so harsh? She surely didn't deserve such unkindness.

Any more than Kathy deserved to be orphaned.

He slipped into bed and pulled the covers to his neck, but lay staring at the darkness of his room.

He could only do his best, even if his best had never been enough to protect his family.

He would not let himself care about another person. He'd never marry and take on more responsibility.

Kathy had been hurt by so many people. He must remind her Winnie was only here a month, warn her not to get fond of her.

Next morning, he prepared to walk Kathy to school when Uncle Mac burst into the house. "Derek, the cows are in the feed stack. I need a hand getting them out."

He hesitated. By the time he returned from the school, the cows would have trampled the stacks into bedding.

"I can stay home?" Kathy seemed pleased with the thought.

"Aren't you practicing for the Christmas concert? Seems you need to be there."

She whimpered. "Don't make me go."

"Derek, come on. I can't do this on my own." Uncle Mac waited with his hand on the door. "Winnie, could you take her to school today?"

Kathy wouldn't go to school on her own. But Derek didn't want her learning to depend on Winnie. Wasn't that what he'd decided just last night? Yet Uncle Mac couldn't get the cows out by himself. Derek couldn't be two places at the same time.

Winnie watched him, her eyes knowing and patient, as if she read his uncertainty.

He'd shared too much the previous evening. Given her reason to think she understood him. He composed his face to reveal none of his confusion, and turned to Kathy. "Would you go with Winnie?"

Her face wrinkled, ready for a good wail.

"Just this one time." He hated to turn her over to anyone else.

"I would love to see your schoolroom," Winnie said. "Do you have some work to show me?"

"The teacher hung a picture I drew on the wall."

"Would you show me?"

"I guess."

"Good. That's settled." Uncle Mac opened the door. "Now let's get those cows back where they belong."

Derek hesitated a moment.

"Say goodbye to your brother," Winnie said softly.

He knew her words were meant for him. Telling him to say goodbye to Kathy.

"I'll meet you after school and walk you home," he promised.

Kathy nodded, and he had no choice but to join Uncle Mac.

By the time they chased the cows back and fixed the broken spot in the fence, he was sweating from exertion.

He glanced toward the house. "I should have let her stay home until I could take her."

"She'll be fine with Winnie. That young woman has her head on solid. She's good with Kathy. Just what she needs. Just what we all need."

"Hardly."

"Take off the blinders, my boy. She's a good looker—"

"I never said she wasn't." She'd cleaned up real good from his first glimpse of her climbing, bedraggled, from the hay. "That's not the point."

"She's efficient."

"I guess so."

"And steady. Why, I bet she would be loyal to the death."

"All I need is someone else to worry about."

Uncle Mac faced him squarely. "What you need is to stop taking yourself so seriously."

Winnie crossed the yard on her way back from school and went into the house, her step light, as if she had not a worry in the world.

Derek knew better. She had no home, her family was lost to her and what she owned fit into a small bag. She should be weighed down with uncertainty. Was she so simpleminded she didn't realize it?

Uncle Mac must have read his mind. "She's learned to enjoy the present without worrying about the future."

Derek snorted. "Sounds irresponsible to me."

The older man sighed deeply, obviously frustrated with Derek. "Like I said, you take yourself and life too seriously. Sometimes I get the feeling you think you need to tell God how to rule the world."

Derek strode away. If he said what he thought, his uncle would likely have a fit, but it seems God didn't take care of things the way He promised to.

Winnie had tried to stay uninvolved with Kathy's angst as they trudged toward school. But Kathy kept glancing over her shoulder.

"Derek will pick you up after class," she assured the child.

"What if he forgets?"

Winnie laughed softly. "As if he would. He'll never forget you."

"Something might happen to him."

Winnie had stopped and squatted to eye level and grasped Kathy's shoulders. "Bad things happen. I can't pretend they don't. But you can't change the future by borrowing worry from tomorrow and trying to carry it today. All of us can only live life one day at a time."

Kathy's dark eyes considered Winnie.

Winnie pressed her point. "You miss out on the good things of today by worrying about tomorrow. Hardly seems like a good idea."

Kathy looked back toward the farm. "I can't see the house."

Winnie realized Kathy was a few inches too short to see the peak of the house. "Would you feel better if you could see it?"

"I'd know it was there."

* * *

By the time Winnie returned home she had an idea. She dug into a box of rags and pulled out a bit of heavy denim, then headed for the barn.

She found Uncle Mac outside, pounding nails into a raw-looking plank of wood. For some inexplicable reason, she did not make her request to Mac. "Where can I find Derek?"

"Try the pen over there." He pointed down the alleyway. "He was working with one of the young horses. Give out a call so you don't startle them."

"It can wait."

Mac scrubbed at his whiskered chin. "Whatever is on your mind was enough to bring you out here, so you might as well get it done. 'Sides, Derek needs to think about something besides work and responsibility. I'm thinking you might be able to nudge him in that direction."

She wrinkled her nose at him. "That's not exactly what I had in mind."

Mac waved her away. "Don't stop an old man from dreaming dreams."

"Even if I tell you it's impossible? Not what either of us wants?"

"Could be the good Lord brought you here for such a thing as this." He pounded on a nail, making any protest useless. She shrugged and headed in the direction he'd indicated. What difference did an old man's opinion make? Didn't change anything. Any more than her wishes had changed anything in the past. Or Derek's worries could prevent troubles in the future.

Ahead, beyond the wooden rails, Derek's voice came to her, calm, reassuring, just as when he talked to Kathy. Safe, sheltering. Her steps slowed, she dragged her mitten along the rough wood, catching and ripping off slivers, tempting them to stab her, yet knowing pain and blood from an injured finger would not ease the emptiness sucking at her soul. She stood stark still, dropped her hands to her side and drew in air, cool, laden with the scent of animals and snow off the mountains. She let the air settle deep into her lungs, holding it until she'd leeched it of all oxygen. Only then did she let her breath out, and keep within her the strength it had given.

She had no one. She needed no one. Especially not someone who resented another person in his life. She did not need his gentle words. His calm assurance. All she wanted was enough money to continue her journey to Banff.

She'd given her word to stay until the Faringtons arrived.

Her conscience dictated she help Kathy as much as she could. Perhaps that's why God had brought her here.

Not because of Derek, as Mac suggested. *Lord, use me, protect me, help me.*

Strengthened by reality and determination, she called out, "Derek, are you there?" and waited for his response.

Silence filled her ears. Then he answered. "Hang on

while I release the horse." A moment later he vaulted the fence. He dragged his gaze over her and glanced beyond her.

"Is something wrong?"

"No. Kathy got to school safely. I met her teacher and saw the room. Admired her drawing. She has a nice touch with crayons and paper. Even the teacher said her drawings were expressive."

He leaned against the fence. "You came here to tell me that?"

It wasn't her purpose in seeking him out, but she was happy enough to relieve the concern he couldn't hide.

"I do have another reason for being here." She explained what she had in mind.

His eyebrows climbed toward his hairline, but before he could voice an opinion she was certain would be contrary, she added, "What does it hurt? And it might help."

He shrugged. "I'll have to get the ladder."

She followed him to a shed where he pulled out a ladder, then she trotted after him to the house and watched as he nailed the flag of denim to a pole and attached the pole to the peak of the house.

"She should be able to see that from the school. It will give her something to watch."

Derek climbed down and stood beside her, staring up at the flapping, faded blue material. "You think it's enough to get her to walk home alone?"

"I can't say. It will take time for her to get over her fears." She refrained from pointing out that he and Mac seem to feed them, rather than give her tools to deal with them. "At the very least, she can look out from the schoolyard and know the house is still here, and by association, assume you and Mac are here as well."

"Seems too easy."

"Sometimes the answers are easier than we anticipate."

He faced her, his eyes full of dark intensity, seeking answers to questions he hadn't voiced—perhaps that he didn't even have words for. "Is that how you see life?" He made the idea sound silly.

"I know life is complicated—"

"Unpredictable? Uncontrollable?"

His driving questions scraped her nerves. She preferred to believe God controlled things. "Personally, I don't want to see the end, the turns in the road. I think if I did, I would live in constant fear."

"You mean like me?" His voice carried a low warning, informing her he didn't care for her evaluation.

She decided to turn the conversation in another direction. "I was thinking of Kathy. Living in fear doesn't change what might come. It only robs you of enjoyment of good things."

"I prefer to call it caution."

She ached to have him understand the difference between the two. Longed to see him know peace. "I learned some hard but valuable lessons. I wouldn't have chosen to be taught by them, but I also don't intend to waste what I've learned."

His look silently demanded an explanation. She

couldn't tell if he wanted to understand, or simply to hear her answer so he could refute it. *Lord, You have taught me to trust You even in difficult circumstances. If there is some way I can make him see it's possible, then use me, guide me.*

"I prayed for a home, instead God gave me contentment. I asked for love, instead He gave me peace. I tried to find my family, asked Him to help me. I found no clue of where they had gone, but I found instead, satisfaction in knowing I am loved by God. That is more than enough."

"I don't believe you."

His blunt words hammered at her self-assurance. She clung with deeply embedded fingernails to what she said. "You're accusing me of deceit?"

"I think you've deceived yourself if you believe you are content and happy to be homeless, with no family and alone in the world."

His accusation tore her fingernails away, leaving her heart in shreds. He had excavated a truth she couldn't face. It was too hurtful, too destructive.

"Believe whatever you want." She congratulated herself on keeping her voice gentle, revealing none of the pain pulsing through her. "I know God loves me. What more do I need?" So much more she couldn't face. "Be sure and tell Kathy to watch for the flag and take comfort in the fact that the house is there. You and Mac are here, too." She turned and headed indoors.

"Winnie, I didn't mean to hurt you. I'm sorry."

She gave no indication that she heard him.

* * *

Why had he pushed her so hard? What benefit was there in poking at her wounds? In making her acknowledge their pain? He should have quit prodding before he made her bleed.

As he returned to gentling the young gelding he'd bought in the fall, he tried to think how to undo what he'd done. Not that he didn't believe she was hiding her real feelings.

But by the time she clanged the metal triangle to signal dinner, he still didn't know how to explain he hadn't meant to inflict pain.

What *was* his intention? To make her face the truth.

Why? Would he feel better if she worried as much as he did, if she bemoaned the facts of her life?

No. He had come to admire her optimism, perhaps even relish it. But it also accused him. Made him aware of his own shortcomings in trusting God, and that in turn made him defensive.

He followed Mac into the house, stood at the doorway and studied her for some indication of how she felt.

She flashed them both a smile. "Soup's ready. And biscuits hot from the oven."

He let his breath ease past his teeth. So she was willing to overlook his comments, perhaps even pretend he hadn't spoken them? His relief was short-lived. She was a warm person, but only on the surface. Below the gentle smile and kind words was a heart frozen with denial.

How was that better than him worrying?

Mac tossed his hat and gloves onto the narrow bench by the door and shed his coat. "Sure does smell good. A man could get used to being greeted by a warm smile and tasty food. Right, Derek?"

Derek snorted. Uncle Mac was anything but subtle, but protests would only encourage him. "Sure could."

Mac grinned and rubbed his hands together as if he'd succeeded in convincing Derek that Winnie was the answer to all their problems.

Derek knew better.

But he was grateful to enjoy the food and the comfortable atmosphere.

Later that afternoon, he strode down the trail to the schoolhouse to get Kathy. She raced out and joined him in the schoolyard. Her eagerness at seeing him erased the tightness lingering in his thoughts from his unkind words to Winnie. This little sister was his life. All that mattered. He turned her toward the house. "Can you see home?"

She shook her head. "Not until I'm almost there."

"Look again. I think you might be able to."

She giggled. "I'm still not tall enough." But she followed the direction of his finger when he pointed. Her eyes widened. "What is that?"

"It's a flag hanging on the end of the house." He made it sound like it was his idea. "Winnie thought of it. Said you might feel better if you could see where the house is."

Kathy clung to his hand and rocked back and forth

on her tiptoes. "I can see it now." The awe in her voice said it all.

How had Winnie known how important this was to his little sister? Why hadn't *he* thought of doing something? A confusion of gratitude and regret twisted his insides.

They headed home. The whole way, Kathy kept her gaze on the flag. Her breath whooshed out when she could finally see the house. "It's right on top."

"Just like I said." He realized not seeing the house had created unnecessary worry for her, and his regret dissipated. Maybe he could find other ways to help Kathy.

He followed her inside.

Winnie waited with milk and cookies. Her welcoming smile faltered a fraction as she saw Derek behind Kathy. "Do you want a snack, too?"

"Sure. Thanks." He didn't normally stop for a mid-afternoon snack, but she seemed to think the idea was okay.

Winnie put out more cookies, asked if he wanted milk or coffee. He chose the latter. Then she turned to Kathy. "Did you see the flag?"

"Right from the school."

"She likes it," Derek added. "Thanks for the idea."

"I'm glad it helps." He sought her eyes. The air shimmered with tension. Then she blinked, and her barriers were firmly in place.

He didn't know which was stronger—disappointment at her withdrawal, or relief to be allowed to retreat to his own safety.

Winnie wanted to ease bedtime both for Kathy's sake and Derek's. Plus anyone else who might be within the sound of Kathy's cries. Everyone was exhausted from listening to the nightly struggle, when she fought her fears and Derek tried to calm her. Seeing the picture at school Kathy drew had given Winnie an idea.

The first thing she needed was blank paper. She found a stack of folded brown store paper in a closet—along with a trunk full of yarn and yard goods.

She folded and stitched the pages together down the fold line to create a little book. She used Kathy's crayons to color the cover and she put Kathy's name on the front.

Winnie spoke to Derek as the little girl put on her nightgown. "I have a few ideas about how to make bedtime easier. Do you mind if I try them."

He gave a lopsided grin. "I'm willing to try anything, and if your idea works as well as the flag…" He shrugged.

Kathy came out, her face already tense.

Winnie took over. "Kathy, I was so impressed with your drawing at school. I told Derek how wonderful it was. I think you have a gift." She hoped to do far more than encourage an interest in drawing. "I made you a little art book." She showed the brown paper book to Kathy. "I think you have time to draw something tonight."

"Before bed?"

"What's wrong with that?"

"What will I draw?"

"Whatever you like, but if you need a suggestion, why not think about your day and draw something that shows the best part of the day for you?"

Kathy put her stuffed bear on the table and picked up a crayon. "Does it have to be something good?"

"Do what you want."

She drew a big black circle.

Winnie sat across the table and Derek stood behind Kathy, watching over her shoulder. Winnie felt his tension, wondered if Kathy did, too. "Why a black circle?"

"That's what bedtime feels like."

"Why?"

"'Cause I'm afraid."

"Maybe we can think of something to put inside the black circle to make it happy instead of scary."

Kathy looked intrigued. "What would *you* draw?

Winnie felt Derek's quiet study as she picked up a red crayon and drew a heart inside the black circle. "This heart stands for love, to remind you that Derek and Uncle Mac love you, and so does God." She met Derek's gaze then, managed to ignore her shock of awareness at the surprise and gratitude in his eyes. "What would *you* draw, Derek?"

He shook his head. "I'm not good at this sort of thing."

"You must be able to think of something."

He studied the drawing a moment, then picked up a pink crayon. He made a circle, added eyes and a smiling mouth, selected a brown crayon and drew hair on the head. "This is Kathy. Thinking of her makes me happy."

Kathy giggled. "I don't look like that."

"A heart doesn't look like that either." He touched the red heart Winnie had drawn.

"It's a val'tine heart," Kathy said with utmost sincerity.

"Now it's your turn," Winnie said to the child, hoping she would think of something to help her overcome her fears of the dark.

"Just one thing?"

Winnie laughed. "As many as you want."

Kathy grabbed a crayon and bent her head over the page.

Winnie shot Derek a glance and saw he was as amused by Kathy's enthusiasm as she. Their gazes collided. In her heart, something burst free. Hope. Her lungs caught on an inhalation. Hope had left her too often disappointed. She lowered her eyes, pushed things back where they belonged and concentrated on Kathy.

After a few minutes, Kathy lifted her head and pushed the book forward for the others to see. "It's a flag. This is my teddy bear. This is Derek."

Winnie chuckled at the long-legged stick figure with

more hat than head. There was another stick figure—a woman, if Winnie guessed correctly. "Your mother?"

Kathy shook her head. "You."

"Me?"

"You said to draw things that make me happy."

She made Kathy happy? *But I'm not staying.* She swallowed the words, rather than steal any of Kathy's contentment. Instead, she patted Kathy's head. "Thank you." And before anyone, namely Derek, could offer a comment, she hurried on. "I really liked it the other day, when you sang that song. Do you remember?"

"You mean—?" and she started to sing the words. "I sing the mighty power of God…." She sang it clear through.

"I like that."

Kathy smiled. "Me, too." She pushed away from the table and turned to Derek. "I'm ready to go to bed." She took his hand and led him away.

Derek shot a look over his shoulder. Winnie almost laughed at the doubt wreathing his face. He came back ten minutes later. "I can't believe it's that easy."

"It might not be. Her fears won't automatically disappear in one night, but given time…"

As if to prove her correct, Kathy's scream filled the air.

Derek bolted to his feet and came back with Kathy in his arms. He cradled her in the rocking chair. His eyes filled with desperation as he met Winnie's gaze across the room.

Oh Lord, calm her fears.

"Derek?" Kathy managed through her tears. "Sing Mama's song."

Derek nodded and began the song Kathy had finished a short time before. She sighed back a sob and fell asleep in a matter of minutes.

Derek carried her back to bed, then joined Winnie in the kitchen. "Still better than most nights."

"It's a start. Give her a few tools and she'll figure out what works for her."

"I guess I should thank you." He walked to the window and glanced out, then turned and faced her.

She wasn't sure what the look in his eyes meant.

He grabbed his coat and rushed out of the house.

Her heart followed him into the cold. How hard it must be to watch his sister struggle with her fear and loss, and to feel so powerless to do anything.

If she could help even a little, she would gladly do so, then walk away with a clear conscience that she had done what she could, and perhaps what God was calling her to do.

At the idea of walking away, her rib cage tightened until she hunkered over against the pain. She had never found leaving easy, but this time she vowed she would do so without feeling as if her world was crashing down around her feet.

God help her. She would do so.

But even as she prayed for protection against involvement, she knew she had already crossed a line in her emotions. And not just with Kathy. She only hoped she could backtrack when the time came.

Chapter Four

Derek strode to the barn. He needed to think. He leaned against the pen and stared at the horse without any purpose in mind but to sort out his feelings.

"Whatcha' doing here, son? Is Winnie settling Kathy?"

Derek jumped as Mac spoke at his elbow. He'd forgotten his uncle was still in the barn. "Kathy is already sleeping."

"Really? What did you do?"

"Nothing. It was Winnie." He described the drawing book and the song.

Mac let out a long sigh. "That's good."

He understood his uncle's relief at knowing Kathy's distress was short-lived tonight. "Kathy's getting too fond of Winnie. She's going to be hurt when she has to say goodbye." His insides twisted. He should send Winnie away now. Before Kathy got any more attached. Before any of them did.

"I think you're missing the point. Even if she cries when Winnie leaves, Winnie's help will still be with her. Son, from the first day when she helped Kathy realize your mother would enjoy seeing her laugh, to this afternoon when she hung the flag, that young lady understood more of Kathy's problems and how to address them then we have in over a year."

"No doubt you mean that to be comforting."

"It's not?" Uncle Mac's voice was low, not expressing any opinion, though Derek was certain he had one. "This is the first night Kathy has settled down in less than an hour."

Derek banged his palm on the plank. "Why didn't I think of doing something different? I'm supposed to be the one who gives her what she needs."

"Sometimes a person is too close to the problem."

Derek suspected Mac meant more than helping Kathy settle for the night, but he wasn't going that direction.

"Maybe God sent Winnie to us for just this reason— to help us know how to deal with Kathy. My advice? Take the gifts she brings and don't worry about what will happen when she leaves."

"I suppose you're right."

"You know I am." He clamped his hand on Derek's shoulder. "I'm hoping you'll see I'm right for more than Kathy's sake."

Derek stared into the dark recesses of the barn. "Don't be hoping on my account. I will never marry."

"So you say. In fact, if you've said it a hundred times, you've said it a thousand—you don't need the responsibility. 'Course what you mean is you're afraid of getting hurt."

Derek jerked away and headed for the door.

Uncle Mac didn't understand that what Derek feared was failing yet again to protect those under his care. As to being hurt when Winnie left…he kind of guessed he had already stepped into that territory. But Uncle Mac was right about Winnie helping. He could live with knowing each day made saying goodbye to Winnie harder to contemplate, if having her stay helped Kathy.

He paused in the cold air and looked up at the stars. No snow tonight. The early snow of October and November was long gone. Maybe they'd have a brown Christmas.

Christmas. His stomach churned. He no longer anticipated the season, full now of painful memories of those gone, and a burning sense of helplessness. His father would be disappointed at Derek's failure to take better care of the family.

Uncle Mac joined him. For a moment, neither spoke; and then the older man said, "Come on, son. Let's see if Winnie has any raisin pudding left."

He let himself be led indoors. Would Kathy still be asleep? Blissful silence filled the room.

"Not a peep from her," Winnie said. A bundle of bright objects lay on the table before her.

His gaze riveted to the shiny red ball. He'd been four, his father still healthy, when Pa lifted him to the tree and helped him attach the ball, then stepped back. "Now it's

Christmas." Derek would never forget the specialness of that day.

He forced his gaze from the red ball but continued to stare at the pile of Christmas things. They hadn't celebrated much last year, still recovering, as they were, from the deaths of three family members. He hadn't thought to do anything special this year. A gift or two, but that's about all.

"Got any more pudding for two hungry cowboys?" Uncle Mac said.

"Certainly." Winnie put out two generous portions. "Tea?"

"Thanks. We'd appreciate some." Uncle Mac gave Derek a funny look. "Sit down. Take a load off."

Derek's knees seemed to have forgotten how to work, and he had to concentrate on lowering himself to a chair as he fought the memories associated with Christmas. The season was supposed to be happy, but his thoughts were laced through and through with regrets, loss and a deep sense of failure.

Would he ever again enjoy Christmas?

Winnie poured tea and sat across from him. "I found these ornaments and wondered what special traditions you have."

Derek swallowed hard and shifted his gaze upward to look at her. Her face fairly glowed with pleasure. He struggled to focus on her question.

"I remember when I was a boy," Uncle Mac began. "Your father was a little gaffer." He nodded at Derek to make sure Derek understood who he meant. "I was probably twelve or so. There were three girls in between us. We lived on a dirt-poor homestead in Kansas. Not a tree in sight. I remembered big pine trees in Grandma and Grandpa's house. But little Georgie had never seen one. I told my parents we had to have a tree. My pa was gone three days and came back with a tree no more than two feet tall. I don't know where he found it, but he'd dug it up rather than cut it, and after Christmas we planted it outside. Would you believe that thing grew? Every year, we decorated it."

Derek had heard the tale before, but still enjoyed it.

"What a lovely story," Winnie said.

"The folks are gone now, but my sister and her husband live there." Uncle Mac got a faraway look in his eyes. "The tree must be twenty feet tall or more by now. I wonder if they still decorate it."

Derek felt Winnie's gaze on him, felt it burn past his memories to a depth in his heart he wasn't aware of. He pictured himself sharing Christmas with her.

This year only.

He stuffed back a twinge of regret. Realized she waited for him to say something. He plucked the red ball from the pile. "I remember—" He told them his memory.

"It was the last Christmas my father was well." Suddenly he recalled something else. "But Pa always wanted me to hold up the youngest child and have her hang the red ball. Everytime, he would say, 'Now it's Christmas'."

Her eyes filled with warmth and she sighed. "That's so special."

Did he detect a hitch in her voice? Something invisible seemed to pass from his heart to hers. A shared enjoyment of the story, but more, perhaps a shared acknowledgment of the pain of disappointment. His had a different path than hers, but he understood she must have watched family gatherings from the sidelines and dreamed of belonging.

He was equally certain she would deny it. No doubt she'd tell him how eager she was to get to Banff and the job there. They both understood her stay was temporary.

"Kathy was the youngest, wasn't she?"

Her question jolted him back to the conversation and he nodded.

"So you held her up to hang the red ornament on the tree since she was tiny?"

"Every year since she was born." He fell silent as he recalled the exception.

"Didn't have much of a Christmas last year." Uncle Mac sounded woeful.

"I was thinking," Winnie spoke softly, slowly. "Perhaps we can make Christmas special this year. Incorporate some old traditions like this red ball, but add new ones so it's less of remembering the past and more about facing the future, enjoying the present."

Derek wanted to protest. He simply didn't have any enthusiasm about celebrating a day filled with bittersweet memories.

"I wouldn't have any trouble finding a pine tree," Uncle Mac said. "I'll take Kathy with me."

"That's a wonderful idea." Her gaze jerked back to Derek before he could sort out how to deal with this latest interference from a temporary housekeeper. And before he could deny the tangle of regrets over knowing she would leave.

He should have known from the first she would find a way to upset their lives. Only, he didn't regret the things she had done. After all, so far they had been for Kathy's good. Even this latest suggestion was meant for Kathy. He could hardly protest. Even though he knew every time she spoke—earnest, concerned with Kathy, full of cheer and good humor—she gained a larger portion of his heart. He seemed powerless to prevent it.

"Mama used to make popcorn on Christmas Eve, and we always read the Christmas story. The children were allowed to stay up late." He grinned. "I think the adults hoped they would then sleep a little later Christmas morning."

Uncle Mac pushed aside his empty bowl and yawned hugely. "Speaking of staying up late…it's my bedtime. I'm going to leave you young ones to plan Christmas."

Derek waited for his uncle to leave the room, then turned to Winnie, a question burning on his lips. "Do you have memories from when you were a child and lived with your family?"

She jerked back, sat up straighter. Her expression flooded with denial.

Before she could answer, he pulled back his question. "Never mind."

Then she smiled and her eyes glistened. "I remember the year my mama made me a rag doll. I felt so loved."

How could parents give a child away? He would protect Kathy with his very life, and she wasn't even his child. But being her brother and the stand-in for her parents, he guessed it was almost the same.

Winnie recovered her usual focus on others. He was beginning to suspect it was her way of escape. "So Uncle Mac will take Kathy to get a tree, you'll help her hang the red ball and I'll make popcorn. Any other suggestions?"

He knew she meant in regards to Kathy, but he had other intentions. "You seem set on proving you don't want to be part of a family."

She grew so still, he wondered if she even breathed. Her mouth was narrow and straight. Then she sucked in air until he thought her lungs must have a hole in the bottom. She released her breath slowly. "In case you haven't noticed, I am *not* part of a family. I have learned to accept that fact and not let it rob me of enjoying life."

"By making everyone else's family work like clockwork?"

Her eyes narrowed. "If I can help someone, why would you consider that a problem?"

He studied her. Saw the pain behind her eyes she

didn't manage to hide. Knew she would deny it if he mentioned it. "I don't...I guess."

They regarded each other like wary combatants.

Then she laughed. "Why are we arguing? I only wanted to talk about Christmas preparations. If you want to turn anything into a tradition, that will be up to you. I'm won't be here next Christmas."

He wondered if he again glimpsed a flash of pain behind her steady gaze.

"My only wish is for Kathy—and you and Mac—to have a special time."

"I'd do anything to make Kathy happy. So—whatever you suggest." He would have no objection to seeing Winnie enjoy the season as well. But how? The one thing she needed despite her denials, he could not, would not offer her.

He would bid her goodbye December twenty-seventh, when the Faringtons arrived.

Winnie looked out the window. Mac and Kathy were out getting a tree. They would all decorate it tonight. The skies were heavy. Perhaps they would get snow. A white Christmas would help make for a perfect holiday, and she was determined to make this the best Christmas ever for Kathy.

Winnie turned from the window and rearranged the decorations, awaiting the time to hang them on the tree.

She picked up the red ornament. Recalling Derek's story of what this ball meant to his family filled her with sweetness that crowded at her careful boundaries. What a special memory of his father.

She pushed the trinket away and strode to the kitchen.

Derek had no right to remind her she wasn't part of a family or to suggest she truly wanted to be. God had seen fit to make her a solitary young woman. She would not let bits of longing and loneliness turn life's joys into dust.

She would not be sucked into the bottomless barrel of wanting what she couldn't have.

Trouble was, her heart did not obey her mind.

She quietly shut out the treacherous thoughts. Come December twenty-seventh she would be on her way to Banff.

Kathy burst through the door. "We got it." Her voice was shrill with excitement.

Behind her stood a tree. Winnie laughed. "Did it walk here on its own?"

"Uncle Mac brought it."

"I don't see him." She did her best to sound puzzled.

Kathy turned and giggled. "He's behind."

"You're sure?"

"I'm here." Mac's voice came from the tree.

Winnie gasped. "A talking tree."

Kathy giggled some more. "Trees don't talk."

The tree pushed into the room and Uncle Mac leaned it against the wall. He dusted needles from his coat. "She went and picked the fattest one in the forest."

"It's the best tree ever." Kathy sighed her pleasure.

Derek stomped his feet on the verandah floor and stepped into the open doorway. "Nice tree, Kit Kat."

"I know. This is going to be such a good Christmas. I can hardly wait." She flung herself at Derek. He caught her and lifted her to his chest.

Winnie's breath caught halfway. She tried to look anywhere but at Derek, but lately her eyes had developed the habit of seeking him whenever he was in the room. Seeing his love for Kathy did funny things to her heart. Made it feel mushy. He was a man who would never shirk his commitment. His strength provided Kathy with more security than he could begin to imagine. He was the sort of man a woman could safely depend on.

She turned away to recapture her wayward thoughts.

A pot of thick soup simmered on the stove. She had brownies baked and hidden in the cupboard—as a treat to go with hot cocoa when they decorated the tree later.

Her self-control firmly in place, she turned to the others.

"Can we decorate now?" Kathy begged.

"Sorry, Kat, Uncle Mac and I have to do chores before dark."

"Aww."

"I'll tell you what. We'll set the tree in place, so as soon as we've eaten we can get right at decorating. How does that sound?"

"I guess I can wait." Kathy managed to pour a great deal of doubt into her words.

"I've got a pail of sand ready." Uncle Mac headed outside.

Derek looked around for a place for the tree. "How about by the window?" He sought Winnie's approval, catching her with her heart too close to the surface.

His eyes narrowed as if he'd read things she could not admit.

She steeled herself to reveal nothing but excitement over Christmas. "What do you think, Kathy?"

"I'd be able to see it when I'm outside, wouldn't I?"

"Sure could." Derek didn't take his eyes off Winnie.

She looked out the window but couldn't stay focused on the distant scene. She allowed herself to glance at the tree. Nice tree. It would look good decorated. Forbidden, her gaze shifted directly to Derek's dark, steady eyes. She couldn't pull away, any more than she could deny she found there something she'd ached for for many, many years.

Slowly he smiled, his teeth a flash of white against his weather-bronzed face.

Her heart split in half and long-denied, always forbidden emotions burst forth. She scrubbed her lips together as her throat tightened with—

No. She only wanted to make this a good Christmas for Kathy. And then she would continue as she'd planned.

No regrets. No pain. No wishing for things that couldn't be hers.

He must have read her determined withdrawal, for his smile soon faded.

She pressed her lips together more tightly and told herself she didn't feel abandoned.

Uncle Mac returned with the pail and the two men struggled to get the tree in place with Kathy's eager help.

Winnie was grateful she had a few moments, unobserved, to get her thoughts and emotions under control.

Satisfied, the men stood back to admire their work.

Kathy clapped her hands. "Now go do chores."

Uncle Mac chuckled. "What's the hurry? I thought I might have a nap first."

Kathy grabbed his hand. "Oh, please, Uncle Mac. Hurry so we can decorate the tree."

Uncle Mac made a great show of yawning and stretching. "It was hard work getting that tree home."

"Uncle Mac." Kathy dragged the words out.

Derek swung her off her feet. "He's teasing you. We're going out right now. You want to help?"

The words were barely out of his mouth before she dashed for her coat and stood bouncing from foot to foot as she waited.

Uncle Mac chuckled and grabbed his outerwear.

"Think she's having fun yet?" Derek murmured as he passed Winnie.

"Not a bit," she replied.

As soon as the door closed behind them, she collapsed on a chair and buried her face in her hands. *Oh, God, help me. All I want is to give them a good Christmas, help them move forward. Oh, and please, God, let me be able to leave without leaving behind my heart.*

They had never eaten supper in such a hurry, and Winnie promised she would leave the dishes until after the tree was done.

She stood back as Derek handed Kathy decorations and helped her put them in place. The red ball was pushed to one side.

Kathy gave a gold bow to Uncle Mac. "You have to help, too." She handed a wooden toy soldier to Derek.

"You, too." Derek carried a silver metal icicle to Winnie.

She shrank back. Being part of this event would only make it harder to keep herself distanced from them. She shook her head.

But Derek didn't retreat. His eyes filled with dark determination and soft kindness. He wasn't about to take no for an answer, so she took the icicle and slowly circled the tree, pretending to look for the best place.

Uncle Mac and Kathy were too occupied to notice, but she felt Derek's watchfulness, even as he continued to hang ornaments.

She blindly hung the bit of twisted metal. She would not let him guess how difficult this was, how she knew she would not leave without tearing her heart from her chest, leaving it bleeding on the doorstep. But leave she would. She must.

"Do you remember this?" Derek asked as he picked up the red ball.

Kathy nodded, her eyes wide.

Winnie ventured a guess the child had forgotten to breathe.

Kathy took the ball and waited for Derek to lift her so she could hang it high on the tree.

The three of them admired the tree.

Kathy sighed. "Now it's really Christmas."

Winnie hung back and watched. This was what she had wanted to accomplish—help them return to the joy of the season—and if it exacted a price from her, she would not complain.

Kathy turned to Derek. "Do you remember Mama's favorite Christmas song?"

In his rich baritone, Derek sang, "Joy to the world! The Lord is come."

Kathy joined with her thin child's voice. After a few bars, Uncle Mac added a quivery, uncertain sound.

Derek reached out and pulled Winnie to his side. Warm, sheltered, she sang with the others. For just this moment, she would let herself be part of a family. As if she really belonged.

Her voice caught on the words, but she forced herself to continue. Derek's arm tightened across her shoulders and she knew he had heard the strain in her throat.

She slipped away as soon as the song finished. "Anyone for cocoa and brownies?"

The four of them hunkered around the table. It was Saturday, so Kathy was allowed to stay up late.

A sudden memory of childhood flitted across Winnie's mind—just a flash, like a bird startled from an overhead tree branch. She stiffened, tried to capture it, identify it. It hovered, teasingly, then fluttered away. She let out the breath of air she hadn't realized she was holding.

Derek reached across the table and cupped his hand over hers. "Something wrong?"

She shook her head, avoided looking directly at him, lest she see kindness and concern. Such a look would bring the tears. She must never start to cry, for if she did, she would never stop.

"Guess what I'm going to draw in my book tonight?" Kathy asked. It had become a nightly ritual, one that seemed to give them all pleasure as they shared both good and bad from their day.

Kathy opened the pages and drew a big Christmas tree. No surprise there. Nor the prominence of the red ball and four stick people with circle mouths. "To show them singing," she explained.

Then she drew four more stick figures. It seemed two were children—a boy and a girl. The other two adults—a man and a woman hovered above the tree.

"It's Mama, Papa, Peter and Susan having Christmas with us," she said, still concentrating on her drawing.

Winnie felt the waiting stillness of Derek and Uncle Mac matching her own. Would Kathy react to this reminder of her loss?

But Kathy continued to work. Finally, she leaned back, allowing them to see what she'd done. She framed the picture with little drawings of the ornaments and star shapes. "Snowflakes," she explained.

Again, something tickled the edges of Winnie's brain. She grew still, waiting, hoping for the thought to reveal itself.

There was a snowstorm. She remembered that much but no more.

Kathy yawned.

"It's time for one little girl to go to bed," Derek said. "Run and get your nightgown on."

Kathy opened her mouth to protest, then smiled. "I guess I am tired."

Winnie stared at the table before her. The memory had retreated, she realized with a sigh of gratitude.

Derek reached for her hand and she knew he had again been aware of her shift of emotions. Rather than let him touch her, she grabbed the empty cups and stacked them together.

Kathy returned and went to Derek's side. "Are you going to sing Mama's hymn to me?"

It had become another part of the nightly ritual.

"If you'd like."

Kathy hugged and kissed Uncle Mac good-night, then went to Winnie's side to do the same. "Thank you for making Christmas so much fun," she whispered.

Winnie blinked back the moisture in her eyes. Despite her best resolve, she had grown exceedingly fond of this sweet child.

Derek took Kathy to the rocker and held her while he sang. She fell asleep in his arms and he carried her into her room.

Restless, Winnie went to stare out the window. A few fluffy snowflakes drifted toward the ground.

"Maybe we'll get snow for Christmas." Derek stood close. She felt him in every pore. Solid as a rock.

Again, the shadow of a memory flickered. She concentrated on the falling snow, willing the memory to the surface. It was so close. She could almost touch it. She shivered, both afraid of the memory and hungry for it.

He draped an arm across her shoulders. Perhaps he thought her shiver meant she was cold. At his touch, her heart reacted like an overexcited puppy. She should pull away. But she didn't.

"I want to add my thanks to Kathy's. You've made the season one to remember."

She could only nod mute acknowledgment.

She would have to fight hard to forget this season, but forget she must, or turn into a mournful woman.

Chapter Five

The stillness of the night wakened Derek. He slipped from his bed, ignoring the iciness of his room, and padded to the window. Snow. Enough to cover the ground and still falling, promising a perfect Christmas.

Not too long ago he'd dreaded the day. Now, he was almost as eager as Kathy. Thanks to Winnie, he realized he had memories to cherish and carry with him, and an opportunity to create new ones.

Winnie had done so much for him. *Them*, he mentally corrected. Kathy especially.

He recalled the many things she'd done to make their lives more pleasant. He wanted to do something in return. Somehow make the day special for her as well. But what could he do?

He suddenly smiled and returned to bed, but as soon as it was light, he tiptoed out to the barn, selected the appropriate piece of wood. He would honor the

Lord's day and wait until Monday to start work on his project.

Kathy waited as he opened the door. "Did you see the snow?"

He shook flakes from his hat to her face. "You mean this wet, sticky stuff?"

She squealed and ducked behind Winnie when he threatened to shake his coat at her.

"It's beautiful out," Winnie said.

Uncle Mac came from his room yawning. "Who can sleep with all this racket?"

Kathy bounced across the room. "Snow. Snow. Snow." She danced to Derek's side. "Let's go play in it."

"Breakfast is ready." Winnie smiled at Kathy's enthusiasm.

"After breakfast. Pleeease." She dragged the word out for ten seconds.

Derek pretended he had to contemplate the question, but the truth was, he couldn't think of any excuse. Playing in the snow with his baby sister sounded just fine. Especially if they could persuade Winnie to join them.

He forced himself to eat slowly, calmly. But something inside him felt as bouncy as Kathy, who teetered precariously and impatiently on the edge of her chair.

The meal over, she dashed for the door and pulled on woolen pants and coat. "Hurry up, Derek."

He shifted his gaze to Winnie. She watched Kathy with affection and maybe just a touch of longing. He couldn't say if the longing took the shape of wanting to belong to a family, or regret at knowing her stay was almost over. But before he got lost in questions he couldn't answer, he spoke. "Winnie, leave the dishes for now and come enjoy the snowfall."

"I'll do them," Uncle Mac offered. "I've enjoyed the scenery often enough. I think it's your turn."

She hesitated a moment, glanced out the window, then smiled. "Sounds like fun."

Kathy raced ahead, dashing from one side of the trail to the other, picking up handfuls of snow, tossing it into the air and letting it fall on her upturned face.

Derek and Winnie laughed.

He took her mittened hand and swung their joined hands.

"There's something about snow."

"You sound as if you aren't sure you like it."

"Oh, it's beautiful. Like a gossamer curtain over the land. But…" She paused. "Something about snow has been tugging at my mind since last night. It's just out of reach. I wish I could recall what it is." Her voice cracked. "Or maybe I don't."

"Sometimes when I push too hard to remember or forget, it makes it impossible to do so."

She laughed. "You mean if I forget about it, I'll remember?"

"Something like that."

"So I need to forget to remember? Or is it remember to forget?"

"Yes."

She jerked his hand. "Oh, you! You're talking in riddles."

He burst out laughing, which brought Kathy to their side.

"What's so funny?"

"Winnie can't remember if she is supposed to remember or forget something."

Kathy shook her head. "That's silly."

"Indeed it is." He tried to make his face appropriately disapproving, but knew he failed.

Winnie's smile caught him in his solar plexus with its gentle sweetness. Despite the sorrows and hardships of her life, she found ways to pour happiness into the lives of others. A true blessing to those she came in contact with.

Kathy grabbed his hand and begged him to play. They started a game of tag that included Winnie despite her protests. She squealed and raced away when he reached to tag her. He easily overtook her. She stumbled as she tried to escape. He caught her, pulled her close, safe in his arms.

Her breath came in gulps. She rested against his chest until her breathing returned to normal, then she stepped back. "Thank you," she murmured, her gaze lowered.

"My pleasure." His voice had a husky note. He cleared his throat, hoping she would think the cold or snow or exertion caused it. Not a foolish desire to hold her close, keep her safe....

He turned away. He was a miserable failure at keeping his loved ones safe.

Kathy danced by Winnie. "Can't catch me. Can't catch me."

With a speed that surprised both Kathy and Derek, Winnie caught her, trapping her in her arms. Kathy wriggled, trying to escape, while Winnie tickled her and wouldn't let her go.

They both tumbled to the ground in a tangle of arms and legs and giggles.

Derek stared down at the pair, his hands jammed to his hips in mock scolding. "How am I supposed to know whose turn it is?"

They stilled and stared up at him. A second too late, he saw the flash of mischief in Winnie's eyes and the way she squeezed Kathy's hand. Before he could back away, they each grabbed an ankle and yanked. He went down like a tree tackled by an axe. His lungs emptied with a whoosh and he lay staring at the sky.

Kathy plunked to his chest and grinned.

"Two against one. No fair."

"You're bigger."

"Can't say I feel a lot bigger lying on the ground with a half-pint gal on me."

Winnie crept closer, on her hands and knees. "We didn't hurt you, did we?"

He groaned. "I think I busted a rib. Maybe two." He groaned again for good measure.

Winnie knelt beside him, her face wreathed in concern. "Should I get Uncle Mac to assist you to the house?"

He snaked out a hand, grabbed one of her wrists and

yanked so that she tumbled to the ground. She grunted and flipped to her back. "You tricked me."

"Guess that makes us even."

Kathy flopped from his chest and rolled to the ground, cuddling close. Winnie lay at his other side, their shoulders barely touching. He stared up into the falling snow, blinking when it landed on his eyelashes. If not for the cold seeping into his limbs, he might be tempted to stay as they were—peaceful and content.

He pushed to his feet, untangling from Kathy's clutches. "I think we'd better go inside and get dried off." He pulled Winnie up and kept her hand in his. He grinned when she made no effort to pull away.

Christmas Eve was on a Sunday, so the church had decided to do the Christmas evening service a week prior to the actual date. Kathy had been bouncing around all afternoon, as if she could make the time go faster by her efforts.

Winnie put the last touches on the cake she would be bringing for the tea after.

Uncle Mac wandered in and out all day, as restless as Kathy.

Derek pretended to read the stack of month-old newspapers, but his mind followed Winnie's movements back and forth. Would she like what he planned to make her? Receive it in the spirit in which he gave it?

And what spirit was that?

Gratitude, he insisted to his mocking mind. Well-wishes for the future. Nothing more. Absolutely nothing more.

He tossed the paper aside.

Winnie gave him a startled look.

"We need new papers," he muttered.

She glanced at the clock over the sofa. He sought the same escape. "Time to get ready."

Kathy dashed to her room. He took his time going to his.

A few minutes later he emerged, a little self-conscious, in his black suit with his new black Stetson. Kathy stepped from her room in a green velvet dress. "Where did you get that?"

"Winnie made it for me." Kathy twirled to show him her dress from every angle. "She did my hair, too."

"Looks good." Brown ringlets tied back by a green bow. "When did she get time to do all that?"

Winnie entered. "It wasn't that difficult."

His eyes widened. Normally Winnie wore a simple frock, which she kept covered by a generous apron. Normally she wore her hair in a simple bun thing, or with braids wrapped about her head and pinned in place, but now... Now she wore a dark red dress with wide sleeves. Now she had her hair parted in the middle and somehow fashioned in rolls behind her ears, making her eyes seem wider. In fact, she was downright attractive. And no doubt every young buck in the territory attending the Christmas service would take note.

A flare of protectiveness seared through his veins.

He would be kept busy keeping them away from her tonight.

She backed up, glanced down at her dress. "Is something wrong?"

"No. You look fine. Real fine."

Pink color pooled in her cheeks. "Thank you. So do you."

He turned away as his own face burned. "Where's Uncle Mac?"

"At your service," Mac called from the doorway. "Your ride awaits."

Derek indicated Winnie should go first and reached for Kathy's hand to follow. Winnie stepped outside and gasped, "A sleigh."

"Thought it appropriate for the occasion."

Derek wondered if there was enough snow for the runners but decided it didn't matter. He sat in the middle with Winnie on one side and Kathy on the other. Mac took the reins. Mac had found buffalo robes and Derek covered them with the warm furs.

"This is really like Christmas, isn't it?" Kathy's voice was filled with awe. "I don't see how I'm going to wait one more week."

"Some of us still have things to do," Derek said. He wasn't anxious for the days to fly past. But time did seem to speed up. The trip took far less time than normal.

After Winnie took the cake to the fellowship hall beside the church, they crowded into the sanctuary with most of the community and found a spot big enough for three of them on the end of a pew.

"I'll sit back here." Uncle Mac indicated the pew two rows behind.

They squeezed in, but Derek didn't mind. He liked having both Winnie and Kathy close and safe.

Kathy left after the congregation sang several Christmas hymns. She'd been disappointed she wasn't chosen to be Mary, but Winnie had made her understand Christmas would be pretty dull if there had been only Mary— "No donkeys, no sheep, no shepherds. It would be so empty."

"She's anxious to be a shepherd now," he whispered to Winnie, breathing in the scent of her hair as he leaned close. She smelled as fresh as the snow, as clean as water in the mountain rivers and as sweet as sunshine on a spring meadow.

He pushed his attention back to the front of the church, where one of the older boys began to read the Christmas story as the younger children performed a silent tableau. Well, no doubt it was supposed to be silent, but one little boy dressed as a lamb kept bleating. His shepherdess continually whispered for him to hush. Her whispers grew louder and louder until Derek could hardly keep his amusement silent.

Winnie pressed her hand to her mouth. Her eyes watered with suppressed laughter.

Finally, a red-faced mother marched to the front and jerked the ear of the innocent lamb, who put on the most injured expression Derek could imagine was possible.

Beside him, Winnie shook with silent laughter and

squeezed his hand as if she needed to hang on in order to keep from breaking out in loud guffaws. He choked back his own laugh.

And then Mary and Joseph entered and knocked on the paper door. Belatedly, someone off-stage hollered, "Knock, knock."

Derek clamped his fist to his mouth. The fact that someone behind him laughed aloud didn't help his self-control.

"No room. No room." The innkeeper was a red-headed boy with a brown dressing gown bundled at his wrists and drooping on the floor.

The rest of the story proceeded with further amusement, and when it ended, people laughed and clapped.

Winnie pulled her hand from his. She slipped from the pew and headed down the aisle.

He glanced after her. No doubt going to help set up tea. She always sought ways to assist, to make others happy.

Not that he was objecting. Except there was a tiny argument niggling at his thoughts.

Who made *her* happy? Or was she as content as she wanted him to believe? It burned at the back of his throat to think she might not be. He had eight more days to do what he could to give her a taste of happiness—something to carry with her. A memory she could cherish.

The congregation began to move to the fellowship hall. He joined Uncle Mac. Kathy waited for them at the door. Inside the hall, the crush of people made it impossible to locate Winnie. It took several minutes for people to settle themselves at the tables.

Derek glanced about. Winnie wasn't dispensing cake, making tea or pouring water for the children. Perhaps one of the bachelors had latched onto her. He looked around the room again, prepared to take her away from any man who thought to claim her. But he didn't find her in the crowd.

"Have you seen Winnie?" he murmured to Uncle Mac.

"Saw her leave the pew and head outside. Haven't seen her since." He gave a quick look around the room. "She's not here."

"I'll find her." He told Kathy to stay with their uncle and strode toward the door.

The air outside was a cool relief to the crowded room. Behind him rose the murmur of voices, but two more steps took him into blessed quiet. A muffled sound to his right pulled his attention that direction. Two lads, too old to be in school, too young to be smart, hunkered down over something. Derek turned away. He didn't even want to know what they were doing.

He strode past them, walked around to the front of the church where a lamp shone on the small crèche scene. That's when he saw Winnie kneeling in the snow before the manger, her hands pressed to her face. Her shoulders seemed to move up and down. Was she crying?

With a muffled protest, he hurried to her, knelt at her side and pulled her hands from her face. He touched his finger to her chin and tipped her toward him. Silvery droplets clung to her lashes. He wiped them away with his thumb. The warmth of those salty tears raced along his blood stream and pooled in his heart, crashing like waves of the ocean. "What's wrong?"

She shook her head.

How could he stop her sorrow if he didn't even know what caused it? He pressed her to his shoulder. "I don't want to see you cry."

"I'm done."

"Done or not—"

She shifted toward the manger. "I remember what I wanted to remember about snow. Only maybe I wanted to forget."

He squeezed her closer.

"Snow was falling the day my parents sent me away. I remember looking back and seeing the light in the windows through a veil of snow. I thought I was going to my aunt and uncle's for a special treat. When I got there they told me I had to stay. They said my parents had no room. No room for me." Her voice wavered.

He clamped down on his back teeth until they hurt. How could anyone treat her so callously?

"I thought I would stay with my aunt and uncle, but my new step-aunt said they didn't have room for a child who wasn't theirs. No room." She sobbed once and quieted. "They had no room for baby Jesus either."

She sat up and pulled away from his arms, leaving him helpless. "I won't feel sorry for myself. I'll make my own room." She spoke with determination.

He touched her chin and gently turned her to face

him. "You don't have to. There's room with us. Marry me." It made such perfect sense, he wondered why he hadn't realized it from the first.

She blinked, wiped her eyes and stared at him. "What on earth do you mean?"

His smile was one-sided. Was it so hard to contemplate life with him? "Marry me. It's the perfect solution. It would provide Kathy the stability she needs. And it would give you a home."

"What would it give you?"

He cared enough about her to want to keep her safe. The best way he could do that was keep her close. "Figure I'll be happy knowing you and Kathy are taken care of."

She sat up and studied him closely.

He met her gaze steadily. He had nothing to hide. He hadn't offered her love. Only safety and security. Love was going too far. He couldn't do that.

"I recall you saying you didn't want the responsibility of marriage."

"Maybe I've changed my mind."

She continued to study him, her gaze searching his eyes, examining his cheeks, his chin, his mouth and returning to his eyes. "Aren't you afraid of the risks?"

"Didn't you once say we should leave the future in God's hands?"

He hadn't exactly said he was prepared to trust God. Better to take whatever steps he felt were necessary, and marrying Winnie was the only way he could think to keep her safe. His answer seemed to satisfy her for she nodded. "I'll marry you and do my best to make you happy."

He nodded. "Thank you." Considered her sweet, trusting face. "May I kiss you?"

"Of course." She turned to him and he gently claimed her lips. He did not linger, though. Neither of them needed to get the wrong idea about the marriage they had agreed to.

Somehow Winnie made it through the rest of the evening. She must have answered questions correctly, taken part in conversations and held her teacup in an acceptable fashion, because she didn't notice any raised eyebrows or startled looks. Derek stayed close. One thing she could be certain of was his protection.

Neither of them had spoken of love. She didn't expect he would. His only reason for offering marriage was to give Kathy a permanent caregiver.

Her only reason for agreeing was to give herself a permanent home where she would always be welcome.

She wanted no more. Expected no more.

She would never give him cause to regret his offer. And she would never be so foolish as to expect or demand love. A tiny, almost unheard voice, one she almost managed to ignore, whispered she didn't deserve love.

They had decided not to say anything at church and to wait until morning to tell Uncle Mac and Kathy.

As soon as Kathy had settled for the night, Winnie slipped away to her own room to think. She opened her

Bible and searched the scriptures for assurance she was doing the right thing. She turned to the Christmas story in Luke, chapter two. She got as far as "There was no room for them in the inn," and stopped. It was the phrase that had sent her shivering into the cold to kneel before the manger.

She'd cried out her heart to God. Why did no one have room for her? Despite her brave words and determination, she longed for a place where she belonged. She'd begged God to help her. That's when Derek had knelt at her side.

She closed the Bible. She had to believe God had sent Derek, prompted his offer of marriage in answer to her prayer. Comforted, she prepared for bed and fell asleep almost instantly.

"You're going to be my mama? This is the best present ever, and it's not even Christmas yet." Kathy hugged Winnie, then turned to hug Derek. "I knew you wouldn't let her go. So did Uncle Mac. Didn't we, Uncle Mac?"

"I had my hopes for both of you." He hugged Winnie. "He's got a long ways to go yet, but don't give up on him."

"I won't." Though she had no idea what he meant. She thought Derek quite acceptable as he was. If anyone had a long way to go, it was she.

She'd awakened in the night, shivering with apprehension. Would he change his mind and send her away?

Uncle Mac clapped Derek on the back and gave him

an awkward hug. "Wise move, my boy. Wise move. Glad to see you listen to an old man's advice occasionally."

Winnie raised her eyebrows.

Derek grinned. "He's been telling me you're the best thing to ever venture into my world."

"She is," Kathy said. "But we despaired of you ever coming to your senses."

At her resigned sigh, they all chuckled.

Later, after dinner, Uncle Mac went to his room for a nap and Kathy shooed them away. "You two go for a walk and make kissy faces, or whatever you're supposed to do. I have something to take care of."

Winnie laughed, even as she knew the heat stealing up her neck would be visible on her face. She wanted to explain their marriage wasn't going to be like that, but Derek grabbed her hand and dragged her outside. "Seems she has important stuff to attend to. We'd better get out of her way and let her do it."

Winnie's heart kicked into a faster pace as Derek took her hand and led her along the snowy path. They paused at the end of the corrals to admire the snow on the mountains.

"Pa dreamed of bringing the family out west. He hoped he'd make it, too. Maybe the air would have cured his lungs."

She squeezed his hand. "Tell me about your father." Mac had said enough for her to know Derek's father had been ill a long time, and more and more of the family responsibility fell on Derek's shoulders.

"He tried hard not to be sick, but by the time I was

seven or eight, he would come home from work and collapse on the bed. I can't imagine how he managed to drag himself to work every day, sometimes shoveling coal for hours. I think his boss must have felt sorry for him and let him drive the delivery wagon. By the time I was twelve he could no longer do it, and I took his place. I hoped if he could rest he would get better. But he didn't. Uncle Mac said his lungs were shot."

"Some things you can't change." The words were empty, meaningless, but she didn't dare offer what she really wanted to—her assurance she would always stand by his side. The best she could do was lean against his shoulder.

"On his deathbed, Pa asked me to do two things. One was to look after the family. I've certainly failed."

"Because of the accident? You can hardly control the universe. Only God can."

"So why doesn't He?" His words tore through her.

"God hasn't forgotten you."

He shrugged. "I couldn't believe it when I got the news. Uncle Mac went with me to take care of the bodies and get Kathy. It's amazing she escaped without a scratch."

"We should always be thankful for God's intervention."

He stared down at her. "You're right. I'm ever so grateful Kathy survived."

Tension eased from her stomach as he smiled. "What was the other thing your father asked of you?"

"To move the family out west. He wanted Uncle Mac

and me to continue with their plans. Uncle Mac came ahead and got this place ready. Then I came out to make sure things were suitable. Ma and the kids followed." His voice deepened.

"I think your father would be very proud of you."

"You do?"

"Certainly. You've never shirked from the responsibility his illness and death thrust upon you. You've done your best to fulfill his dream of giving them a new life. He would certainly not hold you responsible for things beyond your control, any more than you would hold Kathy responsible for the accident that killed the others."

"Of course I wouldn't. What a dreadful thing to suggest."

"Exactly my point."

He grew still, as if he didn't dare breathe. She prayed he would see the truth in her words—he couldn't blame himself for things beyond his power to control. "I see what you mean." Suddenly he laughed. "I have not disappointed my father." He hugged her. "Thank you. You've given me so much. I wish I could give you more."

"You give me all I need." Perhaps not all she wanted, but she was only now beginning to understand what it was she wanted.

He rested his chin on her head and looked about. "It's a good land. A good place to raise Kathy."

He hadn't mentioned having children of their own.

Of course not. Their marriage was simply a business deal. He did not want more responsibility. Even as she did not want the risk of admitting she loved him.

Chapter Six

Derek turned her to face him and looked so long and hard at her that she lowered her gaze.

"What's wrong? Have you changed your mind?" She wouldn't be surprised if he did.

"No. Of course not." He brushed his knuckles along her jaw. "I'm not the sort to back out of a promise."

She knew that. "I wouldn't want you to feel beholden, just because you said something and later changed your mind."

"The only thing I'm 'holding' right now is you. And I'm thinking it was no mistake you ended up in my barn that night." His fingers lingered at her earlobe, then he cupped the back of her head and leaned close.

She knew he meant to kiss her. Not to seal a marriage agreement. No. This time it was gratitude that she'd landed in his life and proven herself valuable to Kathy's happiness. But she didn't mind. Being valued for any reason made her feel safe. She met his kiss halfway.

His lips were warm. His kiss tentative, gentle. She leaned closer, wrapped her arms about his neck and let her kiss speak her heart.

But then she pulled back, appalled at her own behavior. She'd only meant to inform him she appreciated his kindness. "We should return."

He kept his arm across her shoulder as they walked to the house. Surely, he was only being kind. Protective. He would always be protective out of a sense of duty. He would never guess the simple gesture flooded her heart with impossible longings.

She ached for more than a safe home. She wanted to be loved.

Slowly, she took a deep breath. She would not allow herself to discount the gift Derek had given her—an offer of marriage, a place of permanency—by wishing for more.

They reached the house. He opened the door and they stepped inside. The table was set, china teacups that normally sat far back on the top shelf had been washed and set out. Two of them. Kathy had covered a sheet of brown paper with hundreds of flowers to use as a tablecover.

"Surprise," Kathy called.

Uncle Mac leaned against the door frame, grinning.

"What's the occasion?" Derek asked.

"It's a 'gagement party. Miss Parker at school told us about the 'gagement party she went to for her friend."

Kathy's eagerness fled, replaced by uncertainty. "I wanted to do something special for you."

"What a wonderful idea." Winnie hugged Kathy. "We really appreciate it, don't we, Derek?" She shot the startled man a prodding look.

He blinked. "Of course we do."

"Good. Sit down beside each other and Uncle Mac and I will serve you."

Feeling like a cross between royalty and a Barnum and Bailey circus act, Winnie sat, Derek beside her. Uncle Mac stepped forward as if he'd been coached, and poured tea. Kathy brought a plate of cookies from the cupboard. "I wanted to make some for you, but Uncle Mac said to use the ones Winnie made."

"Probably a good thin—" Derek began. Winnie plowed her elbow into his ribs in time to stop him. "This is fine. Just fine."

They each selected a cookie and took a bite.

Kathy waited, facing them across the table. Winnie sipped her tea, nudged Derek to do the same. She stole a glance at him and wished she hadn't. He looked as awkward as if he'd been dropped into the ladies' home sewing circle. She had to press her lips together to keep from laughing.

Kathy sighed. "I wanted this to be special."

"We'll never forget this, will we, Derek?" Another nudge to his ribs—gentle this time.

"Not as long as we live."

Winnie concentrated on her teacup so Kathy wouldn't guess at how hard she struggled to contain her amusement.

Kathy pulled out a chair and sat across from them, her elbows planted on the table, her chin resting in her palms. "Tell me about getting 'gaged. Miss Parker says it's romantic when the man who loves you asks you to marry him." Kathy sighed dreamily. "Was it romantic?" She pinned Winnie with the question.

"Indeed it was."

Derek sputtered tea and grabbed for his handkerchief to wipe his eyes.

Winnie gave him a narrow-eyed scowl. So maybe he didn't see the romance in sitting in the snow, blurting out an offer to marry, but the way he'd held her, the way he'd tenderly wiped tears from her cheeks, and the gentle kiss, were romantic even if they weren't meant to be.

"Tell me," Kathy begged.

"I think they might want to keep the details private for now," Uncle Mac said.

"Aww."

"I can share one thing." Derek nudged Winnie.

Her heart tightened. Was he going to tell the truth? That their planned marriage wasn't based on romance?

He grinned at her, then turned back to Kathy, leaned on his elbows and got dreamy eyed. "Snow was falling, and each little flake that landed on Winnie's skin looked like a tiny diamond from heaven."

Winnie stared, realized her mouth had dropped open, and closed it. The man had a poetic streak in him. What other talents was he hiding?

Kathy let out an expansive sigh. "That's romantic. Now you have to kiss."

"Kiss?" Winnie tried not to sputter. "Why?"

"Miss Parker said that's how you make the 'gagement 'fficial."

Derek edged his chair closer. "You don't mind, do you?" he murmured in her ear.

He was so close, she saw the ebony lights in his eyes, as well as a healthy dose of teasing. She scrubbed her lips together. A kiss? In public? That would make it official?

Derek took her silence for agreement. He cupped her head with his steady hand and leaned forward. His kiss was firm. Solid. Full of promise.

He eased back and grinned at her.

She swallowed hard. Promise for what? Taking care of her? Giving her a home? She lowered her gaze, lest he see confusion and longing in her eyes.

Derek hummed as he worked on Winnie's gift.

"Good to hear you so happy." Uncle Mac had slipped up behind him unnoticed. The old man had a knack for doing that of late.

"Course I'm happy."

"Thanks to Winnie."

"Yup." Knowing she was staying solved a lot of his worries.

Uncle Mac shuffled off and Derek returned to his work and his happy thoughts.

The past three days had been pleasant beyond expectation. There was something about walking into the house, knowing Winnie would glance up and smile a welcome. Knowing he could expect the same face, the same smile in the future. Kathy had settled down, back to the cheerful child he recalled before the accident.

He and Winnie went for walks in the early afternoon and often again after supper. So far, the weather had not grown too cold for them to venture out. They talked about their past and planned their future. He learned about the homes she'd been in and understood she tried to make herself indispensible so they would appreciate her and keep her.

He sat up straight and faced forward. If any one of the homes had valued her, she would not be here. Seems the bad things in her life ended up a benefit for him. He rubbed his neck, trying to ease the sudden tightness, feeling selfish to be grateful for his sake, when it had cost her so deeply.

Something she'd said echoed in his head. "We never know how God is using the events of our lives. We could make ourselves crazy trying to make sense of things like accidents and injuries. Or we can accept that God is in control, and even if we never understand the whys, or see the good in something that's come our way, at least we can rest in His love and leave the questions with Him."

Tension eased from his neck. He might take a while

to truly learn that lesson, but he intended to start working on it.

The sound of an approaching wagon pulled his attention from his thoughts. Visitors? He didn't see how news of his engagement could have reached his neighbors. With no school for a few weeks, Kathy hadn't been able to tell anyone, and they hadn't been off the ranch since Sunday.

Best go see who it was. He set aside his work, threw a blanket over it to hide it from curious eyes and went outside.

"Hello, Derek. A few days early but Merry Christmas."

"Hello, Sam, Jean. Merry Christmas to you, too. Come on in and visit."

Sam lived further up the river. He jumped down and helped to the ground the wife he had sent for last spring.

As Jean smoothed her skirts, he saw she was in the family way.

A baby. Marriage often resulted in one. He swallowed hard, realized he was staring, then led the way to the house.

"We have guests," he told Winnie, who was already pulling the kettle forward on the stove.

He couldn't take his eyes off her. Would she like to make a baby with him? He hadn't thought of marriage as anything more than having a permanent housekeeper. A way to keep Winnie close.

His cheeks burned as he thought of becoming a real family.

A baby. But wasn't birth risky?

He jerked his gaze from Winnie and his thoughts from treacherous paths. He intended to avoid such risks.

"Sam and Jean, this is Winnie Lockwood, my fiancée," he said, with an air of possessiveness.

"Fiancée? Well, congratulations." Sam slapped Derek's back and shook Winnie's hand.

Jean shyly offered her hand to Derek. He shook it gently, then she turned to Winnie and hesitated. With a little giggle, she hugged Winnie. "I hope you'll be as happy as I am."

Winnie's gaze met Derek's, her eyes dark and bottomless. He couldn't read her emotions. He only knew it felt like an accusation and drove a harsh fist into his gut.

Then she smiled. "I'm sure we'll be very happy." She extricated herself from Jean's arms. "I'm just making tea. Sit and visit."

Sam held a chair for his wife and eased her gently onto the seat.

Derek didn't move. The gentleness in his friend's care was like watching a mare with a newborn foal—a combination of tenderness and responsibility. Seems the idea of a baby made Sam aware of the load he would carry. Though looking at the man, one would think he relished the idea.

Uncle Mac came in and greeted the pair, then Kathy joined them.

They visited over tea and cookies. Jean wanted to

know where Winnie had come from and what brought her to the Adams's ranch.

He waited for her reply, wondering how much of the truth she would tell.

She smiled at him, then turned to Jean. "You might say God led me here. I actually had other plans." She told about her desire to work in Banff.

He hadn't thought of her initial goal. Was he asking too much of her, to give up her dream to marry him?

In turn, Jean told how she and Sam had met at her father's house a year before their marriage. "My brother had come west. He's got a place down by Pincher Creek. Sam wanted details, as he was thinking of moving west. Mother was out, so I served them tea. You might say I liked what I saw."

Sam took her hand. "No more than I."

Kathy let out a long sigh. "It's so…"

He knew she was going to say "romantic". And given half a chance, she'd be asking for details, likely to repeat every tidbit to Miss Parker, who seemed to need to get her adventures vicariously. He didn't want to embarrass his guests. "Kathy, would you pass the cookies again, please?"

Kathy shot him a surprised look, but she must have read the warning in his face, for she clamped her lips together and passed the plate to Jean, who took one.

"These are delicious."

"Derek's favorites," Winnie said.

"So you make them often." Jean giggled, as if Winnie made the cookies specially for that reason.

Ginger cookies. Soft and moist. They *were* his favorite, and come to think of it, seems there were always some to accompany his tea. Did she make them solely for him?

But as Uncle Mac took four more, Kathy—at his warning nod—took one and the guests each took one more, he knew he wasn't the only one who liked them. She liked to please others. Not just him.

Why didn't that make him feel better?

Sam cleared his throat. "We brought you a present. But before I give it to you, I want you to know it's fine to say no."

What sort of gift would a person say no to? Unless…

Sam went outside and returned with a small crate. From inside came excited yips.

Unless—he finished his thought—it was a pup.

"We rescued a pair of puppies from an old man up the river. He was going to drown them."

Kathy gasped.

"Sorry, Kathy, but as he said, he had no use for three dogs. We picked one to keep, but thought you folks might like the other." He faced Derek squarely. "If you prefer not, we're fine with that. Just thought we'd give you first chance at refusal."

Kathy had bolted to her feet and rocked back and forth in front of Sam. "Can we see him?"

"Derek?" Sam asked.

He'd had a dog once. Remembered how much fun it

had been. If this mutt was friendly with Kathy, he might consider the idea. "Let's have a look."

Sam put the crate down and removed the lid. A furry brown-and-black bundle scampered out and turned circles on the floor, as if assuring himself he was free. He saw Kathy and wriggled up to her, whining.

Kathy scooped him into her arms, where he wiggled and tried to lick her.

It was a done deal. No way he could take that bundle of joy away from his little sister, but he needed to ask Winnie her opinion first. He turned to her. She watched Kathy, a smile of such sweetness on her face that Derek forgot his question. She truly cared for Kathy. He'd never doubted it, but seeing how it flooded her expression gave him a wonderful sense of doing the right thing by marrying her.

She jerked toward him and her frank love went into hiding.

He obviously did not warrant the same emotion Kathy did. "Would you mind Kathy having a pup?"

She smiled. "Not at all." She stroked the puppy's head. "He's sweet."

"Can I keep him? Really?" Kathy asked.

"Let me have a look at him." He took the pup and examined his limbs, looked in his mouth and ears, which proved a challenge, as the dog wanted to lick him and almost wriggled from his arms.

Kathy giggled. "He says he's healthy. No need to check."

Satisfied as to the general condition of the animal,

he let the pup snuggle into the crook of his arm, where it snuffled once and fell to sleep.

Sam chuckled. "He knows he's safe."

"Home sweet home," Jean said.

Home. Safety. It's what he wanted for himself, for Kathy and for Winnie. It was enough. Wasn't it?

He passed the pup back to Kathy and she sat on the floor to play with him.

The women turned their attention to talk of Christmas plans.

"I wish I could get a turkey," Winnie said. "It would make a special Christmas meal."

"You can. Tell them, Sam." Jean turned to her husband, her face aglow with love.

Sam's gaze lingered on his wife before he turned to Derek. "You remember that German family that took up a homestead over on Bear Coulee?"

He nodded. Of course he did. He wondered how they would make it. Starting from nothing, with half a dozen kids to provide for.

"They raised turkeys and are selling them. I can tell them to butcher one for you if you like. You just have to pick it up before noon on Christmas Eve day."

At the look of eagerness in Winnie's eyes, he would have agreed to ride to Calgary to pick up the bird. "Tell them we'll take one."

Winnie's smile of appreciation made him feel he had done something special.

He shook his head. All this confusion was only

because he had agreed to more responsibility. First marriage to Winnie, and now a puppy.

He was afraid to think about how many things could go wrong.

Chapter Seven

Winnie had the house to herself. Derek and Kathy had taken the pup, christened Beau, for a walk. The pup would provide Kathy with lots of company. Just what the little girl needed. After all, she'd once had a brother and sister to play with.

Winnie appreciated meeting Sam and Jean. Nice to know there were other young couples in the neighborhood, even if their situations were different. Sam was so in love with Jean, Winnie's eyes hurt to watch how he did his best to anticipate and meet her every need.

And Jean had confided her love for Sam. "My heart can only work the way it should when he's around." She'd laughed. "I'm sure you know what I mean."

Winnie bent over the shirt she meant to finish for Uncle Mac for Christmas. She did know what Jean meant. Despite her fears and caution, she'd fallen in love with Derek. Her love required sacrifice from her.

How was she to tell Derek she couldn't marry him?

She prayed for the right words. For the courage.

She heard Derek and Kathy returning and slipped her sewing basket out of sight. She hoped to surprise them all with her gifts.

The pair burst into the room. Beau raced around, checking to make sure he remembered the place.

"I just thought of something," Derek said. "I need to wire the Faringtons to let them know I no longer need them. Do you want to come to town with me?"

"I need to get popcorn." She had to tell him before they reached town.

"Do you want to go, Kathy?"

"Can I stay home with Beau?"

"If Uncle Mac wants to stay."

Uncle Mac came from his room, his hair tousled from his nap. "Did I hear someone say my name?"

Derek explained.

"I'll gladly remain and watch this pair of youngsters."

"It's settled then." Derek went to his room to get his purse and Winnie scurried to hers to tidy her hair. She paused to look in the mirror and forced herself to take a slow, steady breath. *Lord, give me courage.*

Derek chose the sleigh again. A new snowfall made the road suitable for the conveyance.

She climbed in beside him and let him tuck the robes around her knees. Gave a shaky smile when he paused, his face close enough to kiss.

Only he didn't kiss her. Instead, he flicked the reins and they glided down the road. He'd hung bells on the harness. She settled back, allowing herself to enjoy this ride. The last ride she would make as part of his family.

Her nerves twitched as they neared town. She must speak to him before he sent the telegram. Twice she opened her mouth, but the words wouldn't come.

She squeezed her fists open and closed. *Now.* She must do it now. She reached for his hand to ask him to stop.

He misinterpreted her gesture and turned his hand to twine his fingers through hers.

She closed her eyes and prayed for strength to do what she knew she must do. But her heart grew stubborn and insisted she enjoy his touch, his smile and the way he shifted closer so their shoulders and arms pressed together.

She shuddered at all she must give up.

"Are you cold?" He reached around her to tuck the robe tighter.

"Derek, stop."

He jerked back. "I'm sorry. I thought you were cold."

"No. Stop the sleigh."

He pulled on the reins and the horses stood still, steam blasting from their nostrils.

She mustn't take too long or the horses would get chilled. "I don't think you should send that wire."

He twisted to face her. "To the Faringtons?"

She nodded, wishing she had more courage.

"Why not?" His eyes narrowed. "You've changed your mind, haven't you?"

"I must. You deserve to marry someone you can love."

He contemplated her silently.

She lowered her gaze and studied the buttons on the front of his coat. Big. Black. Her sluggish mind could think of nothing more. "I don't want to tie you into a marriage of convenience."

"Isn't that *my* decision? Perhaps it's all I want. I fully intend to send that wire today." He turned and flicked the reins. "I expect you to keep your word. Just as I intend to keep mine."

Her heart lay leaden in her chest. She had succeeded only in making him angry. What was she to do?

They arrived in town. He stopped in front of the store, jumped down and went around to assist her. She put her hand in his, felt him stiffen. "I'm sorry," she murmured.

His hard expression didn't flicker. "Get the popcorn and whatever else you need. I'll be back as soon as I send the wire."

She got what she came for, put it on Derek's bill and then waited for him without even bothering to glance at anything else in the store. There was no pleasure in even looking. In two minutes he returned, helped her in and tucked the robe around her. He would always make sure she was safe, even if he was angry.

Derek avoided the house as much as possible that evening and the next morning. He wished he didn't have to spend time with Kathy and the pup, forcing him to be in the same room as Winnie. To feel her wish to leave. Was Banff so enticing?

He could hardly wait until he could leave to get the turkey and rode out of the yard at a gallop. He slowed as soon as he was out of sight.

How could he persuade her to stay?

By telling her he loved her.

The words blared through his brain.

Love? He had loved his family and lost them, except for Kathy. If anything happened to her, he would break into a million little pieces.

If he loved Winnie, he'd face the same agony.

He couldn't endure it.

He reached his destination, paid the German and headed home with the turkey, refusing to think any further about love. All he had to do was convince her that a marriage of convenience was the best solution for them both.

No risks.

Except to hurt her by not giving her the very thing she needed. Not a permanent home. Not appreciation. Love.

He shook his head. It was the one thing he couldn't give.

He arrived home and handed Winnie the turkey.

"Thank you." She barely let her gaze touch him before she returned inside.

It suited him just fine. He needed time alone. He headed for the barn.

He must finish her gift tonight. He slapped his hat on his thigh. His gift would convince her they could make memories based on something besides love.

He hunkered down on the wooden seat in the corner of the barn and set to work.

Jesus loves you.

Where had that come from?

The words came again. *Jesus loves you.*

Even when things go wrong?

He sat up and stared in the distance, seeing nothing. His heart waited. His thought stalled. A thousand bits and pieces flooded his brain. Jesus becoming flesh and being born a baby. Jesus coming to the world He made and being rejected. Jesus dying on the cross.

Jesus loves you.

Even though it cost Him His life, Jesus loved him.

He wiped away tears he didn't know he cried until they dripped from his chin.

How did God feel when He sent His son to earth, knowing He would endure such horrible things? What a sacrifice it had been for the Father. All to give salvation, hope and an answer to fears. What a shame if people ignored the gift.

What a waste if he refused to let love into his heart.

He breathed deeply. *Lord, forgive my anger at You. Thank You for sparing Kathy. I give You my future to hold in Your hands of love.*

The cracks in his heart mended, and he could look at the truth: he loved Winnie so much it scared him.

Dare he let her into his heart? Risk loving and losing? Feeling he couldn't protect those he loves?

Could he choose to trust God and accept the gifts sent his way. Like Kathy, Uncle Mac and—

Winnie?

He smiled. He might be a fool at times, but he wasn't a big enough one to throw away the chance to love Winnie.

All he had to do was find a way to convince her.

He returned to work on his project. *Please God, I know I don't have the right to ask favors after I've been so stubborn and prideful, but help me tell her how much I love her and let her be willing to make a marriage between us work.*

He finished his original project and added one more thing. Then he went in for supper.

The house was warm and friendly. Kathy and Beau raced over to greet him. Uncle Mac looked up from the table where he was writing something on a piece of paper and nodded.

Winnie waited for him to look at her, and then smiled, tentatively, as if she expected him to still be angry. When her eyes grew wide, he knew he hadn't been able to hide how he felt.

Now for a chance to explain. Perhaps once the others went to bed, but no one wanted to go to bed early.

Winnie popped corn and they gathered around the tree.

Kathy wanted to sing the Christmas songs she

remembered their mama singing. Derek's heart softened at the memories. It was sweet to have good things in his past.

Better yet to anticipate good things in the future.

They finished singing and grew silent.

Kathy lay on the floor, her head cradled against Beau.

Derek leaned over to look closely. "She's fallen asleep. I'll take her to bed."

"I'm ready to hit the hay myself." Uncle Mac stretched and yawned.

Derek hesitated. He did not want Winnie to leave before he got back. "Wait for me?"

She nodded. He couldn't make out her expression well enough in the dim light to know if the idea frightened or appealed.

He hoped she would think it the latter by the time he finished.

Kathy barely stirred as he slipped her dress off, eased her nightgown over her head and pulled the covers to her chin.

He paused at her doorway to calm his nerves. Now that he had admitted he loved Winnie, he realized how much he had to lose if she didn't return his feelings.

But he would not let fear deprive him of this opportunity.

He stepped into the main room. Ensconced in the wooden rocker, she turned and gave a tentative smile.

"I'll be right back." He grabbed a lantern and trotted to the barn to grab his gift.

Returning, he burst into the house and forced himself to slow down. Suddenly he didn't know how he was going to present the gift, what words would express his heart.

She waited, watching him.

He had to do something, say something. "I made this for you." He placed the present in her lap.

He felt awkward towering above her, forcing her to tip her head to look at him, so he squatted at her knees. "Unwrap it."

She folded back the towel he'd covered it with.

"A box."

"A memory box." He tipped the lid toward her so she could read the words.

"Winnie's Memories."

"I remember you saying how we should keep the old memories and add new ones, or something like that."

She stroked the wood he had sanded and polished to a fine patina. "It's lovely. Thank you. I have something for you, too."

But he held both arms of the chair and trapped her in place. "There's more. Open the box."

She lifted the lid and pulled out a carved wooden heart.

He swallowed hard as he sought for the right words. "It's my heart." He plucked it from her palm. "I give you my heart." He pressed it back into her hand and curled her fingers around it. "I love you with my whole heart. I want to marry you because I love you and want to share my life with you."

The seconds ticked by. She shifted her gaze back and forth from her hand clutching the heart to his eyes. He couldn't read her thoughts. But if he had to guess, he would venture to say he'd frightened her.

"I hope you'll learn to love me. I'm willing to wait for that day. In fact, I want to marry you, love you and take care of you for the rest of my life, even if you never return my love."

She nodded.

He pulled her to her feet, keeping her within the circle of his arms. "There is no pressure. My love is free. No obligation." He wanted to kiss her, but he wanted her to know he would not take advantage of her in any way. "Now, off to bed, and I'll see you Christmas morning."

"Your present—"

"Give it to me then."

There was only one Christmas present he wanted.

He loved her.

Winnie stared into the darkness.

No one ever loved her before. No one except God.

Others had said they did. She recalled her mother saying it and then giving her away. Her aunt and uncle had never spoken actual words of love, but said how precious she was. "A gift from God." Until their own babies came. The others hadn't pretended to love her. She wouldn't have believed them if they said they did.

She didn't trust the words. Far easier to live pretending love didn't exist.

She clutched the wooden heart to her chest.

I give you my heart.

She shook but not from cold. From nerves.

Could she trust love?

Lord, this is everything I've ever wanted, but I am so afraid it isn't real. Or it might not last. Please send me an answer so I know what to do. What to say.

Derek said he was willing to accept a marriage without her love, but it wasn't that she didn't love him.

She was afraid if she spoke the words aloud the dream would vanish.

How can I be sure it won't?

Her thoughts circled endlessly.

She focused on the season. Christmas.

Glory to God in the highest and on earth peace, good will toward men.

Jesus—God in flesh. A gift. To bring us peace. Peace with God. The peace of God.

The words mocked her. She had no peace.

Trust in God.

She did trust God. She had most of her life.

But you don't trust God to be able to work through others. You want only to let Him into your heart.

She had good reason to distrust people.

But if she wanted the one thing she needed—love and belonging—she had to trust God would keep both her and Derek in the palm of His hand.

Was that too much to trust Him for?

She knew the answer to her question. Peace descended and sleep finally claimed her.

* * *

She woke to Kathy calling, "It's Christmas morning! Get up, everyone, so we can open gifts. Hey, where are the gifts?"

The adults had decided not to place them under the tree until morning so as not to tempt Beau to explore.

Winnie dressed hurriedly, as anxious for the day as Kathy, but for an entirely different reason. Scooping up her parcels, she hurried from her room. Uncle Mac and Derek stepped from theirs at the same time, both with arms full as well.

"Merry Christmas," they said in unison.

Winnie laughed. She suspected her eyes overflowed with joy for the day.

"Hurry, hurry," Kathy called.

Laughing, the three of them hurried to the tree and deposited the gifts. Already the smell of the turkey cooking filled the room. She was glad she'd put it in the oven the night before. The aroma made Christmas more real.

Beau caught Kathy's excitement and tore around the room yapping. Derek caught him and held him to calm him.

"Can I open a gift now?"

Everyone agree Kathy should go first. She opened the biggest one, which was from Uncle Mac—a nice bed with a little mattress for Beau.

The next one was from Derek. She folded back the

paper to find a real drawing book with thick, smooth pages. "Ohh, I can hardly wait to draw in it."

Then she took the gift Winnie handed her. She unwrapped a rag doll complete with cherry-red cheeks and black braids, her dress of the same material as Kathy's new dress. "I love her! Thank you." She hugged each of the adults.

"I made everyone something." She passed them each a gift. They opened up drawings. She had not drawn stick figures. In fact, her drawings were quite good. Derek's showed him riding his horse. Uncle Mac leaned against a fence before the barn. Winnie stood in front of the house, the mountains rising behind it. She looked like she was welcoming someone home. Kathy had titled it *"Home, Sweet Home."*

"How lovely. I'll find a nice frame and hang it where I can see it every day. In fact, we'll frame all three of them."

The men had gifts for each other—a new lariat for Derek, a new belt for Uncle Mac.

Uncle Mac gave Winnie a nice serving tray.

She gave Uncle Mac his gift from her. He displayed his new shirt proudly.

The last gift was for Derek. He pulled out a shirt. "It's fine. Really fine." She hoped he was pleased.

"Try it on."

He shook the folds out and a small package fell to his lap. He opened it. Her aunt had given her the small hanging that Winnie had carried with her since she left her uncle's house. The edges were dog-eared, and stained where she had pressed her finger to it many times. "I'm sorry it's not new."

He read the words aloud. "'Many waters cannot quench love, neither can the floods drown it.' Song of Solomon, eight, verse seven."

"All my life I have hoped and prayed for that kind of love. I have found it here. Thank you." She meant to include them all, but couldn't tear her gaze from Derek's dark eyes.

Uncle Mac cleared his throat and pushed to his feet. "Kathy, I think Beau needs to go for a walk."

Winnie barely noticed the pair leave the house, with Beau tearing out the door ahead of them.

Derek slowly rose and stood before her. He pulled her to her feet and held her shoulders. "Winnie, do you mean to say you love me?"

"I certainly do. I've known for a while, but feared to trust it."

"No more fears?"

"God has given me what I always wanted. I'd be foolish to throw away such a wonderful gift."

Derek sought her gaze hungrily. She knew he waited to hear the words—the same words that had melted the resistance in her heart. "I love you, Derek Adams. I will gladly share your life, help raise your little sister and build a solid home here in the west."

He still kept her at arm's length. "Winnie, I promise to love and protect you always. You and any children

God blesses our union with. You have completed my life and given me real happiness."

He finally pulled her close and she lifted her face to meet his kiss, giving her whole heart into their promise.

* * * * *

If you loved this novella by Linda Ford,
be sure to pick up DAKOTA FATHER,
available in January 2010,
only from LOVE INSPIRED HISTORICAL.

Dear Reader,

In an earlier book, *The Path To Her Heart*, I mentioned the tragedy of children taken from families against their will. It got me to thinking of children who suffered even worse—given away by parents because of economic or health restrictions. Thus Winnie was born. Okay, created. I wanted to tell her story but to set it in a positive light. What better way than to give her Christmas?

I love the simple message of Christmas—God's love sent to us in the form of a baby. Yet so often I miss the simplicity of the message as I add commercialism, consumerism and other-isms. Writing this story was a joy because my characters brought me back to the true meaning of the season. Wouldn't it be great if all of us could get down to the basics of love and joy this Christmas? I pray that will be the case in my family and yours.

I like to hear from readers. Contact me through email at linda@lindaford.org or lindaford@airenet.com. Feel free to check on updates and bits about my research at my website www.lindaford.org.

God bless,

Linda Ford

QUESTIONS FOR DISCUSSION

1. Winnie has known rejection. How has it shaped her character? What word or words would you use to describe her?

2. Winnie is on her way to Banff to work in a sanitorium. Why does she feel this is the solution for her problems? Do you agree with her?

3. When she first meets Derek, she is not thinking romance and yet something about the man appeals to her. What is his appeal?

4. Derek is father and mother to Kathy. How is he doing at the job? How does he think he is doing?

5. Derek's faith has been sorely tested by the events leading up to the story. What has his reaction been?

6. Christmas reminds both Winnie and Derek of some important truths. What are they, and how does each character apply it to his/her life?

7. God's love healed their hearts. Do you have a hurt that needs God's love and healing? God is offering it to you today just as He was ready to pour it into Derek and Winnie's life. What truth do you need to grasp?

Love Inspired.
HISTORICAL

TITLES AVAILABLE NEXT MONTH

Available January 11, 2011

THE GUNMAN'S BRIDE
Catherine Palmer

DAKOTA FATHER
Linda Ford

THE DOCTOR TAKES A WIFE
Brides of Simpson Creek
Laurie Kingery

A MOST UNUSUAL MATCH
Sara Mitchell

LIHCNM1210

REQUEST YOUR FREE BOOKS!

2 FREE INSPIRATIONAL NOVELS
PLUS 2
FREE
MYSTERY GIFTS

Love Inspired
HISTORICAL
INSPIRATIONAL HISTORICAL ROMANCE

YES! Please send me 2 FREE Love Inspired® Historical novels and my 2 FREE mystery gifts (gifts are worth about $10). After receiving them, if I don't wish to receive any more books, I can return the shipping statement marked "cancel". If I don't cancel, I will receive 4 brand-new novels every other month and be billed just $4.24 per book in the U.S. or $4.74 per book in Canada. That's a saving of over 20% off the cover price. It's quite a bargain! Shipping and handling is just 50¢ per book.* I understand that accepting the 2 free books and gifts places me under no obligation to buy anything. I can always return a shipment and cancel at any time. Even if I never buy another book, the two free books and gifts are mine to keep forever.

102/302 IDN E7QD

Name	(PLEASE PRINT)	
Address		Apt. #
City	State/Prov.	Zip/Postal Code

Signature (if under 18, a parent or guardian must sign)

Mail to Steeple Hill Reader Service:
IN U.S.A.: P.O. Box 1867, Buffalo, NY 14240-1867
IN CANADA: P.O. Box 609, Fort Erie, Ontario L2A 5X3

Not valid for current subscribers to Love Inspired Historical books.

Want to try two free books from another series?
Call 1-800-873-8635 or visit www.morefreebooks.com.

* Terms and prices subject to change without notice. Prices do not include applicable taxes. Sales tax applicable in N.Y. Canadian residents will be charged applicable provincial taxes and GST. Offer not valid in Quebec. This offer is limited to one order per household. All orders subject to approval. Credit or debit balances in a customer's account(s) may be offset by any other outstanding balance owed by or to the customer. Please allow 4 to 6 weeks for delivery. Offer available while quantities last.

Your Privacy: Steeple Hill Books is committed to protecting your privacy. Our Privacy Policy is available online at www.SteepleHill.com or upon request from the Reader Service. From time to time we make our lists of customers available to reputable third parties who may have a product or service of interest to you. If you would prefer we not share your name and address, please check here. ☐

Help us get it right—We strive for accurate, respectful and relevant communications. To clarify or modify your communication preferences, visit us at www.ReaderService.com/consumerschoice.

LIH10R

When Texas Ranger Benjamin Fritz arrives at his captain's house after receiving an urgent message, he finds him murdered and the man's daughter in shock.

Read on for a sneak peek at DAUGHTER OF TEXAS by Terri Reed, the first book in the exciting new TEXAS RANGER JUSTICE series, available January 2011 from Love Inspired Suspense.

Corinna's dark hair had loosened from her normally severe bun. And her dark eyes were glassy as she stared off into space. Taking her shoulders in his hands, Ben pulled her to her feet. She didn't resist. He figured shock was setting in.

When she turned to face him, his heart contracted painfully in his chest. "You're hurt!"

She didn't seem to hear him.

Blood seeped from a scrape on her right upper biceps. He inspected the wound. Looked as if a bullet had grazed her. Whoever had killed her father had tried to kill her. With aching ferocity, rage roared through Ben. The heat of the bullet cauterized the flesh. It would probably heal quickly enough.

But Ben had a feeling that her heart wouldn't heal anytime soon. She'd adored her father. That had been apparent from the moment Ben set foot in the Pike world. She'd barely tolerated Ben from the get-go, with her icy stares and brusque manner, making it clear she thought him not good enough to be in her world. But when it came to her father...

Greg had known that if anything happened to him, she'd need help coping with the loss.

Ben, I need you to promise me if anything ever happens to me, you'll watch out for Corinna. She'll need an anchor.

I fear she's too fragile to suffer another death.

Of course Ben had promised. Though he'd refused to even allow the thought to form that any harm would befall his mentor and friend. He'd wanted to believe Greg was indestructible. But he wasn't. None of them were.

The Rangers were human and very mortal, performing a risky job that put their lives on the line every day.

Never before had Ben been so acutely aware of that fact.

Now his captain was gone. It was up to him not only to bring Greg's murderer to justice, but to protect and help Corinna Pike.

For more of this story, look for DAUGHTER OF TEXAS by Terri Reed, available in January 2011 from Love Inspired Suspense.

Copyright © 2011 by Terri Reed

SHLISEXP0111

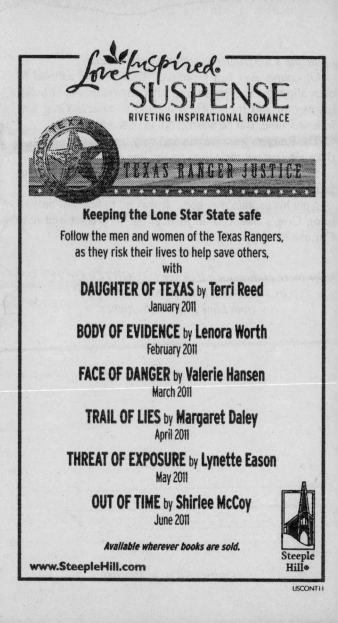

Love Inspired
SUSPENSE
RIVETING INSPIRATIONAL ROMANCE

TEXAS RANGER JUSTICE

Keeping the Lone Star State safe

Follow the men and women of the Texas Rangers,
as they risk their lives to help save others,
with

DAUGHTER OF TEXAS by **Terri Reed**
January 2011

BODY OF EVIDENCE by **Lenora Worth**
February 2011

FACE OF DANGER by **Valerie Hansen**
March 2011

TRAIL OF LIES by **Margaret Daley**
April 2011

THREAT OF EXPOSURE by **Lynette Eason**
May 2011

OUT OF TIME by **Shirlee McCoy**
June 2011

Available wherever books are sold.

www.SteepleHill.com

Steeple
Hill®

LISCONT11